Endorsements

Cleverly thought-out and brilliantly executed, Ruth Leigh bestows upon us the backstories we never knew we needed. Leigh has breathed life into those who made but a cameo appearance in *Pride and Prejudice*. Delightful!

Rose Servitova, author of 'The Longbourn Letters', 'A Completing of The Watsons' and 'A Season at Sanditon.'

'Whether or not you are an Austen fan, you will love these glimpses into the lives of minor Pride and Prejudice characters. With warmth, wit and a detailed understanding of the period, we are drawn effortlessly into the social niceties and small calamities of everyday Georgian life. These are fascinating cameos of minor characters in this timeless book, brought to life with skill and artistry.'

Deborah Jenkins, author of 'The Evenness of Things' and 'Braver' (shortlisted for the Writers' Guild Best First Novel Award).

A GREAT DEAL OF INGENUITY

A collection of *Pride and Prejudice* short stories

Ruth Leigh

Copyright © Ruth Leigh 2023

The right of Ruth Leigh to be identified as the author of this work has been asserted by her in accordance with the Copyright, Designs and Patents Act 1988.

All rights reserved. No part of this publication may be reproduced or transmitted in any form or by any means, electronic or mechanical, including photocopy, recording, or any information storage and retrieval system, without permission in writing from the publisher.

Published by Resolute Books
www.resolutebooks.co.uk

ISBN 978-1-915981-22-6

Dedication

To all Austen fans, everywhere, in the hope that this book finds a home on your bookshelves and a place in your heart.

I wrote this book for everyone who yearns to know more about the world of the Bennets, the Lucases, the Bingleys, Meryton and beyond. I worked from the Penguin Classics 2003 updated version of the novel. It was originally published in 1813 by T Egerton.

Acknowledgements

I wrote most of this book in the early part of lockdown in 2020, struck by the notion that *Pride and Prejudice* is full of characters about whom we know very little. Like so many other devoted Janeites around the world, I absolutely love the novel, and the sheer pleasure of making up back stories about some of its minor characters certainly didn't feel like hard work. When I first wrote the outline three years ago, I was a freelancer with no experience of writing fiction and no belief in my own ability to find a publisher. I am grateful, therefore, to my colleagues at Resolute Books, who invited me to join their authors' collaboration at just the right time. Huge thanks to Sheila Jacobs for her thorough copy edit, to David Salmon for the cover design, to Liz Carter for helping me through the maze of formatting the book online, to my first readers Charlie, Jane and Jenny and as always, to my husband, who is the first person to read every word I produce.

Biography

Ruth is a novelist and freelance writer, the author of the *Isabella M Smugge* series, contemporary humorous page-turners. She lives in beautiful rural Suffolk with three children, one husband and a cat. Ruth has been an Austen devotee since the age of fifteen and is a proud member of the Eighteenth and Nineteenth Century Nerd community.

You can find her on Instagram, Facebook, TikTok and Twitter at ruthleighwrites and at her website, www.ruthleighwrites.co.uk.

Notes on the Text

I have used the spelling prevalent in Austen's time. Hence, 'stile' for 'style', 'chuse' for 'choose', 'neice' for 'niece' and so on.

Where appropriate, there are footnotes to explain words and phrases unfamiliar to modern readers.

Contents

Introduction	1
Miss Gardiner	5
Harriet's Story	18
Sally	34
The Reverend Mr Annesley	55
The Harrington Sisters	85
The Cook's Tale	111
An Unremarkable Woman	126
Mrs Long and Her Neices	154
A Fine Trousseau	186
Bibliography	201
Also By This Author	203

Introduction

Let's go back in time. It is the spring of 1981 in West Essex and copies of Pride and Prejudice are being handed out to a class of fourteen-year-old girls. We are in the first year of our O-levels and so far, the only subjects in which I shine are English Literature and Language. I've heard of Jane Austen, but only via the pages of 'What Katy Did Next'. The heroine Katy Carr is travelling through Europe with her companions Mrs Ashe and her young daughter. When they visit Winchester, an elderly verger at the cathedral is confused by the constant stream of visitors to Miss Austen's grave.

'Whatever was it, ma'am, that lady did which brings so many h'Americans to h'ask about her? Our h'English people don't seem to take the same h'interest.'

'She wrote such delightful stories,' explained Katy; but the old verger shook his head.

'I think h'it must be some other party, Miss, you've confused with this here. It stands to reason, Miss, that we'd have heard

of 'em h'over 'ere in England sooner than you would h'over there in h'America, if the books 'ad been h'anything so h'extraordinary.'

I flicked through my copy. Like the verger, I couldn't see what all the fuss was about. We must have studied the book, but I have virtually no memory of it. A year later, my English Language O-level under my belt, I came across the novel on my bookshelf, opened it up and fell in love. I've been reading it ever since. At the end of March 2020, I was sitting up in bed having a cup of tea and re-reading Pride and Prejudice for the thousandth time. As with all true Janeites, I found something new in each reading, but on this occasion, long on time and short on work, a thought suddenly lodged itself in my brain. At some point in the late eighteenth century, in Meryton, there must have been a pretty, lively young girl living with her family and starting to think about marriage. Her name was Miss Gardiner and she was the reason I wrote this book.

For who knows who Miss Gardiner is? And yet she has her own story. Seizing a tablet of paper and mending my pen (OK, I confess. I opened up the laptop) I wrote her tale at top speed. It opened the floodgates. I scoured the novel for characters who appear only once or twice or who are only alluded to in the course of the narrative. I immersed myself in the eighteenth century, learning about Hertfordshire geography, history and sayings, looking into the background to Austen's writing and dashing off down various rabbit holes in search of interesting facts to underpin my stories. Along the way, I got to re-read some of my favourite Austen scholarly works and remind myself just why it is I love this novel so much. Join me then as we return to Meryton and district to meet some of the figures in the shadows and watch them come into sharp focus.

Miss Gardiner

In some ways, Miss Gardiner needs no introduction. However, have one she must, since she would be the first person to complain of discontent if this were not the case. This story is the only one written from the point of view of a male character and the eagle-eyed reader will spot a myriad of tiny clues as to Miss Gardiner's identity planted throughout the narrative. At this point in her life, she is pretty, merry, good-natured and carefree and it is through the enchanted eyes of her new husband that we now meet her for the first time.

MY WIFE LIES softly sleeping by my side. Up on one elbow, I gaze at her lovely countenance, her tumbled hair, her rosy cheeks, her cherry lips. Yesterday was our wedding day, this morning the first of many joyous ones yet to come. My heart is full.

As long as I live, never shall I forget when first I saw my dearest wife. I had occasion to drive to town on a bright January day to conduct some estate business. Having left my horse and equipage at the inn, I was making my way along the High Street when my attention was drawn by Mr Gardiner the attorney, walking towards me with a young lady on each arm.

We stopped to exchange greetings. 'Allow me to introduce my daughters,' said he. 'Miss Gardiner and Miss Maria Gardiner.' The two young ladies curtsied. The elder looked up at me through long, dark lashes and I fancied I discerned a faint blush on her rounded cheeks.

We walked on together to the haberdasher's where we bade each other farewell. Miss Gardiner glanced over her shoulder as she walked into the shop, catching my eye and blushing again. Her pretty face and sparkling eyes remained in my mind all day and when I betook myself to bed that evening, her countenance was the last memory which remained in my mind before sleep overtook me.

†

The next week, I once again had reason to drive to Meryton. Walking from the apothecary, I espied Miss Gardiner on the other side of the street looking into the window of the milliner's shop.

My heart beating faster, I approached her. I bowed. 'Miss Gardiner. I trust that I find you well?'

She curtsied. 'I am very well, I thank you, sir. A fine day, is not it?' She laughed, charmingly, and my heart leap't.

It was dirty underfoot, with mud on the road. 'Shall we walk together?' asked I, all daring, offering her my arm.

As she turned her face up to mine, I gazed into her fine, dark eyes and my heart beat faster. We talked civilly of the weather, the latest assembly and her family.

'My elder brother has been from home for some time,' said she. 'He is apprenticed to a merchant in London. We all miss him most exceedingly. Our family circle is in sad want of his lively character and wit.'

We strolled on slowly, and by the time we approached the coaching inn, Miss Gardiner's destination, I had learned that she had one older brother and a younger sister (Miss Maria, whose countenance was to me a perfect blank – I seemed to recall that her hair was light, but little else), that her father and mother lived in the house next to the parsonage, and that she was very fond of music and dancing.

'And do you indulge your passion for dancing often, Miss Gardiner?' I enquired. She laughed and shook her head. Her curls danced and her eyes sparkled. 'No, indeed, sir! Indeed not! I find myself dull and without occupation when there is no dancing to be had at the assembly rooms.'

Greatly daring, although I do not often frequent these dances (full of chattering misses and their dumpy mamas), I asked if I might be so bold as to request her hand in a dance when next we met there.

'Sir, I would be honoured.' I felt her little gloved hand tighten on my arm and fixed my eyes on her glowing face, raised to mine. We were now nearly at the coaching inn and

I found myself longing to learn what this beautiful young creature did to amuse herself.

'With what do you fill your days? Are you a great reader? Do you play an instrument? I know that many young ladies are accomplished in such occupations.'

She coloured slightly. 'I confess, sir, I am not a great reader. My father often reads to us in the evening, but left to myself, I would not take up a book when there is dancing or music to be had. I walk with my sister, we help my mother in the flower garden, we sing. We do not have an instrument.'

She hung her head as though ashamed.

I recalled that her father, although respectable, did not have an estate and that he could probably not afford such luxuries for his daughters. 'My dear Miss Gardiner, forgive me! I forget myself. What do you do at the inn? Are you to meet your family there?'

She blushed and smiled. 'Indeed, sir, I am. My dear brother is expected on the coach from London and my mother and father and I are to meet him there. My sister stays at home to make ready for his return.'

We had reached the door of the inn. I longed to spend more time with Miss Gardiner, but propriety forbade it. She turned around as she stood at the inn door, her pretty face smiling and her eyes dancing. 'May I introduce you to my mother, sir? I know she would be delighted to make your acquaintance. And perhaps I might introduce you to my brother when he arrives.'

We walked in together where Mr Gardiner and his wife were sitting by the fire. After the introduction was made,

Mrs Gardiner invited me to sit beside her while her daughter walked to the window to look out for the coach.

†

Mrs Gardiner's voice was querulous, and the contrast between her person and that of her daughter was marked. She began to question me. I knew, of course, that she saw me as a potential suitor for her eldest daughter's hand. I had often been quizzed by eager mamas. As a single man of good birth with an estate and a modest fortune, I was only too aware that I was an object of great interest for many single young women.

While there were many agreeable young ladies in the limited society in which I moved, none of them were handsome or charming enough to tempt me into marriage. My dear mother had begged me not to marry the first young woman I saw and I had borne this in mind, perhaps for too long as I was now nine and twenty and still single. My love of independence kept me from loneliness, but Miss Gardiner's beautiful face and pretty ways were captivating and I found myself thinking of her almost constantly. I believed her to be only seventeen years old, but her position in the family as the eldest daughter had, no doubt, given her the mantle of responsibility, decorum and household knowledge that I would wish my own wife to have. It was from that day in the inn that first I began to picture her as the future mistress of my home.

I answered Mrs Gardiner's questions with patience and good humour. As she was quizzing me about my parents, I heard the rattle of the coach bumping over the cobbles.

'He is come! He is come! Oh, my dearest Edward!' cried Miss Gardiner, clapping her hands prettily and running out of the inn. I was charmed by her impetuous manner and affection for her older brother. I began to make my farewells, but Mrs Gardiner entreated me to tarry and to meet her son.

For a few minutes, all was confusion as the coach stopped and the passengers dismounted. Miss Gardiner came skipping back into the inn arm in arm with a tall, sensible-looking young man perhaps a year or so younger than myself. Once he had embraced his mother and shaken hands with his father, he turned to me with a smile. His mother made the necessary introductions. 'I am delighted to make your acquaintance, sir,' he said in a pleasant voice.

After a few more moments of conversation, I bowed and made my farewells, but not before Mrs Gardiner had invited me to dine with the family in three days' time. I professed myself delighted. I confess that I eagerly anticipated seeing Miss Gardiner in the bosom of her family.

†

I dined with the Gardiners three times that month. It was everything that was charming and hospitable. Mrs Gardiner kept a very good table and a well-ordered household. The young ladies chattered and made merry and I soon began to feel that I was a favoured guest. Sitting opposite Miss Gardiner at table, the soft candlelight reflecting from her bright eyes and pretty face, I was ever more captivated by her.

Alone in my library with the candle guttering in the draught from the window, I considered leaving the single state and entering into matrimony. My excellent parents had died within six months of each other, shortly after I reached the age of one and twenty. My home needed a mistress. Only a wife could bring me the domestic comfort and marital harmony for which I longed. I wished for a family of my own, a son to inherit my estate and perhaps daughters to laugh, and run around, and sing. If I could have a child as merry and captivating in manner as Miss Gardiner, I should have nothing of which to complain. No daughter of hers could fail to be lively, accomplished and sensible.

I resolved to approach her father the very next day and ask for her hand. I flattered myself that she felt real affection for me and would give me the answer for which I yearned.

†

After my solitary breakfast, I bade farewell to the housekeeper, Mrs Hill, and rode into town. Walking up the path to the Gardiners' house, I saw a movement at an upper window. Looking up, I saw the curtain fall as though a hand had let it drop.

I was shewn into Mr Gardiner's book room. He seemed not at all surprised to see me. I declared my love for his daughter and asked his permission to propose marriage. 'My dear sir!' cried he. 'I am all happiness! Please do pay your addresses to my daughter. I have no doubt that she will receive them with pleasure. I think you will find her in the parlour arranging the flowers.'

I walked out into the entrance hall, my heart beating fast. I could hear a soft voice singing in the parlour. My love was standing there with her arms full of fragrant blooms. I will not sport with your patience, dear reader, with the words of passion which flowed from my lips. I will tell you only that after a few minutes, the flowers lay unheeded on the table and I was an engaged man.

†

What sweets then followed. I dined each evening at the Gardiners' and walked with my love in the garden, arm-in-arm. She hung on my every word, fixing her eyes on my face as we talked of our forthcoming conjugal felicity. I had explained to her father the limitation on my estate. 'Pish, sir!' he laughed. 'You will have sons, fine sons, to deal with that.'

I did not doubt it. My love was young, healthy and full of captivating sweetness. I was sure she would bear me many children.

Sometimes, a cloud would pass over her lovely face when I spoke of financial matters. 'My love, do not bore me with such disagreeable things!' she would entreat me, pouting and putting her pretty head on one side. 'Do not you have news of how the house does? Shall we have new paper in the dining room as you promised me? Shall we have a wilderness in which we can walk? I long to hear of it!'

I could deny her nothing.

†

One day, walking in the garden as our marriage day drew nearer, I once again ventured to speak to her about my estate and its financial constraints. I persisted, gently, lovingly, in spite of her protestations. 'My love, we must speak of this. I know 'tis dull, but it is of great import to our life together.'

She pouted and frowned. She spoke pettishly. 'Have you no concern for my nerves? How can you teaze me so?'

Tears filled her beautiful eyes. I tried again to explain to her, but she pulled away from me and ran back to the house.

I reminded myself that my own sweet love was very young yet and ignorant of the ways of the world. That evening, in a quiet moment in the parlour, we embraced and I begged her forgiveness. Never shall I forget the sweet pressure of her lips on mine. A plague on finances! Economy is perfectly useless when we are to be together for the rest of our lives.

†

My love of the country and of books will, I am persuaded, be added to my wife's interests when we are married. The countryside in which sits my house and its grounds is verdant and lovely. I do not expect so young a lady to comprehend all the volumes contained in my library, but surely, we will sit together by the fireside while I read to her after dinner. How delightful it will be to have the opportunity to improve her mind and increase her understanding!

My wife will be settled only a mile or two from her family, so that we may visit them and welcome them to our house as she pleases. I have the carriage in which she may drive into town to carry out her commissions and I have laid in a stock of pretty trifles for her to amuse herself once we are married. I flatter myself that no young lady could wish for more.

I am by nature a solitary being, and I confess that the regular experience of feminine chatter and laughter at the Gardiners' house was not something I wished to prolong. After dinner, Mr Gardiner and I would drink our port and talk of business and of politics while the ladies disported themselves in the drawing room. Mrs Gardiner and her daughters are very fond of fashion, and all three ladies would be amusing themselves by trimming bonnets and caps when we joined them. My own love and her sister would play spillikins[1], while Mr Gardiner and I engaged in games of draughts or backgammon. I longed to have my own dear girl as my wife in our comfortable drawing room, away from the snores of Mrs Gardiner and the shrill giggles of Miss Maria.

News has recently reached me of the birth of a healthy son to my fool of a cousin. His lady gave her own life for that of her child, leaving his father alone to bring up his son and heir. I shall be gracious and invite the child and his father to my house when we are married. Is it wrong of me to picture my own sons, strong and healthy, while my

---

[1] A popular game played with sticks made of wood or bone. The aim is to remove a stick without disturbing the others. These days, it's known as Pick Up Sticks.

mewling cousin cowers inside with the ladies? My own dear love, I know, will welcome my family, however disagreeable they may be, with smiles and warm hospitality.

†

Mr Edward Gardiner is become a particular friend. He is a most sensible and agreeable gentleman, prospering in his trade in London and shewing every sign of becoming a successful merchant. He has been most helpful in arranging my dear girl's trousseau and all the fol-de-rols which young ladies seem to require.

'Edward knows all the best warehouses,' said Mrs Gardiner to me, one fine morning as we sat in the parlour. 'He has been most obliging.'

I trusted that she was not going to speak to me of muslins and ribbons.

She coughed and touched the lace fichu[2] at her throat. 'My dear sir,' she began, rising to her feet and walking to the window. 'Mr Gardiner and me are both vastly pleased that you will soon be joining our family. I could not wish for a better husband for my girl. However, I feel it incumbent on me to mention that my daughter has not been used to being burdened with household cares. She is but seventeen years old and has not been used to thinking on serious subjects. She is the most good-natured girl in the county, but I fear – that is, I wonder…'

---

[2] This was a triangular shawl, often made of lace, worn around a woman's neck to keep out draughts. At a time when houses were heated by open fires, ladies would wish to avoid stiff necks and chills and thus the fichu became a practical, yet attractive feature of Regency costumes.

'Madam!' I cried. 'Your daughter will never know a moment's care when once she becomes my wife. Miss Gardiner is uniformly charming and I anticipate many years of domestic felicity ahead of us.'

'Thank you, sir, indeed, I am excessively relieved,' replied Mrs Gardiner, sinking back into her seat. 'She is very young and inexperienced, but in all other matters, she is the sweetest and best-tempered girl who ever lived. I am sure that she will make you a very proper wife.'

†

The sweet season of our courtship was almost over. Hill and the staff prepared to welcome their new mistress. Each day, I walked around the grounds, overseeing the work of the gardeners whom I have directed to plant sweet-smelling shrubs and plants near the windows so that my love might enjoy their fragrance while we stroll together. Nothing is too much trouble for her.

And so, I lie here in our marital bed, gazing down at the sleeping countenance of my wife. Our marriage day was all happiness, all joy. Even my dolt of a cousin wished us well.

The trees are in blossom, promising a year of much fruitfulness and bounty. Flowers make everything lovely and my bride outshone them all in beauty, her arms full of sweet spring blooms. How my heart leap't when first I saw her walk towards me on the arm of her father. Even Miss Maria made a tolerable bridesmaid, although her incessant chatter grated upon my nerves.

Never shall I forget the moment when first I sat with my wife in the chaise and four, her little gloved hand in mine.

As the carriage began to move, we turned and waved to our family and friends. We trotted along the lane to our home, both of us as happy as 'tis possible to be. 'Well, my dear, and how feel you to be a wife?' I enquired, as I looked down into my love's pretty, blushing face.

'My dear! I am quite overcome. I cannot wait until we reach the house. I am quite wild to see it.'

Indeed, I trust that my dear wife will grow to love my estate as much as I do myself and that many children will come to bless us. Of course, we will soon be blessed with a son to join in cutting off the entail[3] when he is of age, and my foolish cousin Collins will be no more than a family joke. I am filled with love for my dear wife – her youth, beauty and good humour have captivated me, I own. Domestic happiness full of respect, esteem and confidence must be ours for many happy years to come.

My love is stirring. Daylight peeps through the curtains. I smooth her pretty hair back from her forehead and kiss her cherry lips. 'Good morning, Mrs Bennet.'

---

[3] An entailment is a legal way of restricting the inheritance of an owner's property to his lineal descendants under estate law. Longbourn and Mr Bennet's estate can only pass to a legally begotten male heir, but since he has no son, his nearest male relation is Mr Collins. Hence Mrs Bennet's desire to marry one of her daughters to him, which, at a stroke, would ensure security for her as a widow and any of her unmarried daughters.

Harriet's Story

Harriet Forster is first mentioned as the Colonel's rumoured fiancée in Chapter 12. At this stage in the novel, no further information is given, and her very existence may be only the result of some unfounded Meryton gossip. However, shortly after Christmas, at a time when Jane Bennet's spirits are dejected due to Mr Bingley's return to London and the Gardiners have returned home, Mrs Forster, described only as, 'a very young woman' is brought to Meryton by her husband. From a narrative point of view, she is a new character joining a relatively limited society which already contains a number of excitable teenage girls. Kitty and Lydia Bennet, Pen and Harriet Harrington, Maria Lucas and Mrs Long's nieces are all in need of new society and gossip in the dark days of January. Colonel Forster, about whom we know very little, is probably a man in his forties and since Mrs Forster quickly becomes best friends with Lydia Bennet, fifteen at the time of their meeting, she is very likely still a teenager herself. Austen tells us, 'A resemblance in good humour and good spirits had recommended her [Mrs Forster] and Lydia to each other, and out of their three months' acquaintance, they had been intimate two.' This seems to imply that the Colonel's new wife is as silly and empty-headed as Lydia. In the 1995 BBC adaptation of the novel, Mrs Forster is indeed very young and is given little to do except encourage her husband to give a dance. There are tiny clues embedded in the text that she is not as foolish as her friend, and we should also remember that Lydia's elopement with one of her husband's officers would be a disgrace for both the Forsters. The Colonel travels from Brighton to Longbourn as soon as he hears of Lydia's flight, implying that he is a man of honour. In Chapter 47, as Jane is explaining to Elizabeth how they found out about Lydia's elopement, she says of Colonel Forster, 'His behaviour was attentive and kind to the utmost.' He and Harriet are still newlyweds when the scandal erupts in Brighton, and I do wonder how it impacts their marriage.

―――

IT WAS BUT a few months ago that I was sitting in the parlour with Mama and my sisters, weeping, in deep mourning for dear Papa. Our grief was compounded by the certain knowledge that we would be thrown upon the charity of our family. With no brother to support us and only Mama's modest widow's portion, our future looked bleak indeed.

Now I am elevated by marriage, by rank, by, dare I say it, a growing affection for my husband. No longer little Harriet Richardson, I am now a married woman with a loving husband, I want for nothing and am able to assist my dear family.

But I am running ahead of myself.

'My love,' Mama said to me one morning. 'I wish that you would put on your bonnet and walk to the apothecary for me. Eliza's cough is no better and I would welcome some of Mrs Smith's lozenges. The poor child has slept hardly a wink.'

I ran downstairs, put on my shabby bonnet and walking shoes and hurried to the apothecary's. I had put on my bonnet in a great hurry and as I walked down the busy High Street, I did not notice that the ribbon had worked loose. A gust of wind tore it from my head and to my horror, I watched as it fell to the ground and came to rest in a puddle. Tears filled my eyes. Poor Mama did not have enough money to buy me a new one. I would have to be seen with a ruined bonnet until we moved to live with our hateful cousins.

I walked into the apothecary's, my handkerchief to my eyes. As I struggled to choke back my tears, I was startled by a deep voice addressing me. 'Madam, I fear that you are not well. Is there anything I may do to assist you?' I looked up to see a tall, respectable-looking gentleman in full regimentals.

I was overcome with confusion. We had not been introduced.[4]

---

[4] At this time, it was vitally important to be officially introduced to a new acquaintance. The general rule was that the lower status person was introduced to someone of higher status. In this situation, Harriet is very much in the former category. She is a young, unmarried woman and the Colonel is an important man. That is why she is alarmed about speaking to him in the shop and why Mrs Smith acts as the third party in making the introduction. Once this has been effected, Colonel Forster is able to speak to her whenever they meet and be introduced to her mother, who is now the head of the family. Before the introduction has taken place, the Colonel is jumping the gun, socially. He knows the etiquette, but is clearly attracted to Harriet and wishes to know her better.

I blushed. 'Sir,' I stammered. "You are very kind. I thank you. I am quite well, only a little distressed over my poor bonnet.'

He bowed.

He was a great deal taller than myself, and as I looked up at him, I noted that he had a kind countenance, although not at all a handsome one. There were flecks of grey in his hair, and lines around his eyes as he smiled down at me. Confused, I approached the counter to order the lozenges and Mrs Smith promised to send them up to the house directly.

'How do you all do, my dear?' she enquired kindly, pressing my hand. I felt tears rise to my eyes, unbidden. The grief of losing dear Papa was still almost unbearable.

'We are all well, madam, I thank you, but it is hard. So very hard.' My voice shook. 'We go to live with my uncle and his family after Christmas. He is very kind to offer us a home, but I will miss… I do wonder how I will… oh, dear Papa!' At this, I broke down altogether and covering my face with my handkerchief, I gave myself up to my misery. Mrs Smith continued to press my hand and did not irritate my feelings with inconsequential chatter. As my tears subsided, I became aware that the strange gentleman had moved over to the other side of the shop and was absorbed in gazing at lavender water and toilette preparations.

I felt ashamed of allowing my feelings to shew before a stranger. I thanked Mrs Smith and prepared to leave.

'Miss Richardson, do not forget that I have some packages made up for your mama which she ordered last week. But you do not have your basket with you – I can send them up with the lozenges for Miss Eliza if you chuse.'

As I stood, unsure, by the counter, the strange gentleman walked over.

'Would you do me the honour of allowing me to carrying your packages?" he asked. "It is exceedingly wet and dirty underfoot, and I would be sorry to see your parcels come to grief.'

I looked to Mrs Smith for guidance. Dear Mama is exceedingly careful about our behaviour in public. Mrs Smith had known our family for many years, however, and she willingly made the necessary introduction.

'Sir, this is Miss Richardson, the eldest daughter of a respectable family here in Ware. She lives with her mama and three younger sisters. Her papa was a most valued member of the town community, and we all grieve his loss. Miss Richardson is a great comfort to her family.'

My heart beat rapidly and I blushed deeply as the gentleman bowed and introduced himself. I now knew his rank and his name. I looked up into his face.

'I thank you, sir, I would be most glad of your arm.'

The gentleman smiled. His whole face became less craggy and I saw a kindly twinkle in his eyes.

'May I ask you if I might have the great honour of being introduced to your mother?'

He gave me his arm and we walked slowly up the street towards home.

†

That was at the beginning of October. Our new acquaintance, we learned, was the colonel of a regiment quartered in Meryton, around fourteen miles west of Ware.

He had important business with the attorney in our town, necessitating several visits. Mama invited him to dine with us the day after our first meeting on the High Street and he very quickly became a valued acquaintance. His good breeding and amiable manners endeared him to Mama and as a gentleman, he was able to offer us assistance, which as a family of unprotected females was most welcome. My youngest sister Mary, a child of eight years old, became rapidly most attached to him and would run to meet him, laughing with delight, when she saw him approaching our house. He would often bring a pretty trifle to amuse her and my next youngest sister, Anna. They both missed dear Papa exceedingly and would often ask Eliza and myself when he was coming back.

In between his visits, the Colonel wrote to me, with Mama's permission, and his letters were one of the few things to which I looked forward as Christmas drew near.

Our home was no longer the happy, comfortable place it had been when Papa was alive. Mama did her best, but the furniture was shabby, we had been forced to sell many of our possessions, including the instrument on which I had been so proficient, and we were painfully aware of our decreased standing in society.

One morning, I found Mama sitting in the parlour with a letter in her lap and a handkerchief to her eyes.

'I have received this from your uncle, Harriet," said she, passing me the note. "He proposes that your aunt and your cousin Fanny visit us for two days on their way to London to buy Fanny's wedding clothes. I am ashamed for them to see us in this unhappy state, but I cannot refuse them hospitality.'

My heart sank. My uncle and aunt had offered us a home with them as soon as they heard the news of dear Papa's death, but it was done with little compassion and their letter of condolence spoke duty in every line. Their eldest daughter, Fanny, was several years older than myself and had become engaged in the spring. Between Fanny and myself there had never existed a true friendship. When we were children, she would boast to me of her toys and pretty dresses and now that we were both out[5], the difference between us was even more strongly marked. I dreaded her arrival. I knew that she would bring nothing but haughty pride to our home and I felt oddly shy of her meeting our new friend. The Colonel's visit coincided with that of our cousins and I knew that Mama wished to introduce him to them.

Still, there was nothing to be done. We made our home ready for our visitors, and in due course, they came. My aunt walked in to the vestibule and kissed us, remarking that we were much grown since she last saw us. I noticed her cold eye travelling rapidly over the furniture and the faded places on the walls where our pictures had once hung. Fanny walked in behind her.

---

[5] Girls of genteel breeding were kept in the schoolroom until their parents or guardians decided it was time to introduce them into society. When a girl came out, it was a sign that she was ready for marriage. Generally, the age for this was between fifteen and eighteen. A young girl would be able to attend balls and assemblies (suitably chaperoned) and start to attract male attention. It was the usual practice to allow an older sister to marry before the younger came out, the married woman being able to chaperone the unmarried and introduce them to suitable men. The Bennet girls are unusual in that all five are out before any are married.

I composed myself with some effort and greeted my cousin warmly. 'You are most welcome, Fanny. Let me congratulate you on your forthcoming marriage.'

Fanny smiled her gloating smile. 'Thank you, Harriet. Mr Penshurst has made me very happy by asking for my hand. I shall want for nothing.'

There seemed nothing else to say. We stood there for a moment before Mama caught my eye and I remembered my duties. We took tea in the drawing room and then I walked upstairs to my room which my cousin would be sharing with me for two nights. My heart sank at the very notion.

Little Mary came running up to me. 'Harry,' she whispered indignantly, seizing my hand. 'I don't like cousin Fanny. She was rude about Jemima! Why can't she stay at the inn instead of here with us?'

I laughed in spite of myself. Mary was devoted to her doll, Jemima, who went everywhere with her. I could imagine my cousin's pretty mouth twisted in a sneer as she gazed at my little sister's most precious possession. I squeezed her warm little hand and we walked into my room together.

'Poor Mr Penshurst,' Mary continued. 'He will have to live with cousin Fanny forever and ever. She might be rude about his dollies.'

Fanny was cold, snobbish and unkind, but I understood enough of the world to see that men often see a pretty face and do not discover the true nature of the woman they have married until it is too late. I pitied Mr Penshurst who, I hoped, was not marrying my cousin for her yielding manner. I knew her well enough to believe her capable of assuming a prettily behaved exterior, while all the time scheming to provide herself with a good match.

†

Breakfast the next morning was not our usual happy meal. My aunt and cousin sat looking at our plate and silver as though it offended them, and there were many awkward silences.

After breakfast, Fanny announced that she wished to walk into town to look at the selection of ribbons in the haberdasher. I was painfully aware of my old, shabby bonnet with its stained ribbon. Mama had done her best to mend and clean it but I was embarrassed to see Fanny staring at me as we set out. Eliza was to accompany us as Mama believed that a walk and some fresh air would do her cough good. We walked in silence until Fanny began boasting of the house she would live in and the fine carriage in which she would ride out. We took no pleasure in hearing her, but politely assented to all her comments and congratulated her once again on her good fortune.

At the haberdasher we divided, Eliza walking on to call on her friends the Miss Haywards. I stood, blushing miserably as Fanny had Miss Greenwood the haberdasher running hither and thither as she called for ribbons and dress lengths to be brought to her.

'These are vastly provincial, Harriet,' she said loudly, waving Miss Greenwood away. 'In London, Mama and I will be visiting the best warehouses to buy my trousseau. Are not you going to buy a new bonnet? Yours is sadly shabby and unfashionable.'

I saw Miss Greenwood frown at this. I turned from Fanny and started examining some cherry coloured ribbons which I would dearly have loved to buy. The door opened and to my confusion, in walked the Colonel.

He saw me and smiled. 'My dear Miss Richardson! I trust I find you in good health? And your mama and sisters? Are they well?'

I replied that we were all well, painfully aware of my reddening cheeks and the childish stammer which returns to haunt me when I am nervous. Fanny was staring rudely at the Colonel.

'Sir, may I introduce my cousin, Miss Fanny Hetherington. She and my aunt are breaking their journey to London for two days and staying with us.'

The Colonel bowed.

Fanny curtsied and smiled insolently. She turned her head and looked me full in the face. 'Well, Harriet, are you going to buy those ribbons or simply stare at them all the morning?'

I was all confusion. I felt my stammer return.

'I… I do not think that I shall buy them, Fanny. Mama says… that is, I do not need new ribbons.'

'They are a very pretty colour, Miss Richardson.' The Colonel had picked up the ribbons and was examining them in the light by the window. In his large, manly hands, they looked like the silly fripperies they were.

'I do not need them, sir!' My voice sounded louder than I had intended and the Colonel looked surprised.

Fanny was smiling in her sneering manner. 'They would suit you, Harriet. What a shame you cannot afford them.'

I blushed and blushed again. Never had our reduced circumstances felt so shaming to me. I could not bear to meet the Colonel's eye.

There was a short pause then he spoke. 'Would you do me the honour of taking my arm, Miss Richardson? I would very much like to call upon your mother upon my way back to my lodgings.'

Silently, I took his arm and we walked out of the haberdasher's with Fanny following on behind.

†

Dinner was not a happy experience. My aunt and Fanny were coldly civil towards the Colonel and their manner cast a chill over the table. That evening, as we prepared for bed, Fanny leaned towards me, her eyes alive with malice. 'Well, Harriet, it may be that you are not to live with Mama, Papa and me. A situation may arise which will change everything.'

She smiled at me, head on one side, eyes narrowed. I said nothing.

'Come, Miss Harriet, surely you must own that it is almost a settled thing. Your mama would be making a perfectly respectable match. He would not do for *me*, but such an old gentleman would make a very acceptable second husband for your mama. How shall you like having a new papa?'

I could not speak. My feelings were in turmoil and my heart beating so fast that I felt it would leap out of my breast. I had not thought that the Colonel was courting

Mama. A new and painful emotion overcame me. I knew not what to say.

Fanny laughed. 'Are you struck quite dumb, Harriet? Why else would such an old, grizzled man pay visits to this household of women?'

'He is not old,' I stammered, the colour rising into my cheeks. "I believe he is around three and forty."

'Three and forty, is he?' sneered my cousin, slipping off her ruffled dressing gown and dropping it on the floor. 'More than twice your age, but a good match for your poor mama. She cannot afford to be so discerning as I would be. Well, good night, cousin – I wish you a good night's sleep.'

She blew out the candle and I was left to a sleepless night of tears and uncertainty.

†

The next morning, my aunt and cousin departed soon after breakfast. I could not pretend to be sorry that they had gone, and even dear Mama, the kindest and most hospitable of women, sighed with relief as their carriage disappeared from view.

Little Mary was not so polite. 'I hope they never come back again, Harry!' she cried, dancing round the breakfast room with Jemima in her arms. My mother gently chided her, but I could see that her heart was not in the reproof.

A sleepless night had left me tired and with a headache. Mama's perceptive eyes missed nothing in her household. 'My own love, you look tired. Did not you sleep well? Are you troubled?'

I could not stop my tears. Mama comforted me as I sobbed, then I recounted Fanny's impertinent words.

Mama changed colour and her eyes narrowed. 'My dear! I can assure you that the Colonel has no interest in *me*. I respect and esteem him, but I could never marry again. He has not offered me his hand, nor will he. However, your cousin was right in one respect. My dearest girl, the Colonel is in love with *you*, and wishes to ask you to marry him. My child, you are very young, but the Colonel feels sincere affection for you and wishes to make you his wife.'

I was all astonishment. My eighteenth birthday was not until April and marriage and an establishment had not seemed a possibility for me since Papa had died. I had very little dowry. My only fortune was my youth and tolerable good looks. I did not flatter myself that I was a beauty, but I had noticed young gentlemen glancing at me in the street of late and my glass told me that I had pretty hair and regular features.

Mama continued, tears in her eyes. 'I believe your dear papa would have approved of such a match if he had been spared to us. But what think you, dearest Harry? Could you feel affection and regard for the Colonel? Could you consent to become his wife?'

'I do not know, Mama,' I stammered. 'May I have time to think?'

'Of course, my love.' Mama embraced me. 'The Colonel is a kind and good-natured man. I would not be able to part with my dear girl to anyone less deserving. Let us speak of this after dinner once the children are gone to bed.'

I put on my poor bonnet and walking shoes and set off for a long walk along the river bank with its pretty gazebos.

Could it be possible that the Colonel was in love with me? I thought too highly of his kindness to my family to accept him purely for mercenary reasons. True, I would want for nothing, I would be the Colonel's lady, with the power to assist my own dear family and to oversee a household of my own. But could I feel the necessary affection and regard for him, without which I believed it was not possible to enter into even a tolerably happy marriage?

I walked for above two hours, coming to rest upon a bench which looked out over the river. I had promised Mama my answer by nightfall and as yet, I was no nearer knowing what that answer should be as when first she told me of the Colonel's love. In a flutter of spirits, I began the walk back home.

†

I write this on the last day I shall sign my name Harriet Richardson. Tomorrow, I will be Harriet Forster, wife to Colonel Forster. We will leave for Meryton from the church door, as my husband returns to his regiment in the town in the middle of January.

On the afternoon he came to me to ask for my hand in marriage, we spoke of our future together and the changes which would come into my life.

'My dearest love,' said he, as we sat in the drawing room together. 'I know that I will be taking you from your family and to a strange place. Yet Meryton is a pleasant and sociable town, with many families with whom we are on good terms. I hope that you will make some particular friends amongst the young ladies there and soon be on terms of comfortable intimacy with at least some of them. We dine with the Lucases, the Harringtons, the Longs, the Bennets and the Philips, and perhaps a dozen more. Meryton has taken the regiment to its heart, and I am sure that you will find that a warm welcome awaits you. I know that you will miss your sisters and your dear mama, but we are close enough that not half a day's journey will bring them to us.'

My nerves were in a flutter at the thought of leaving all my friends and family and journeying with my new husband to Meryton where I knew no-one. I took comfort from his assurance that Eliza could come and stay with us whenever she wished and that as the sister of the Colonel's wife, she would enjoy many social engagements, balls and dinners which were not possible at home. I also knew that Meryton would be my home only for as long as the War Office wished it. As the Colonel of the regiment, my husband would lead his officers to any part of the country in which they were required. This knowledge had cost me some bitter tears, but a woman must follow her husband and I was tolerably reconciled to the change in my life.

Colonel Forster pressed my hand and fixed his eyes upon my face.

'There is one more thing, my dearest Harriet, before I leave you tonight. With your mama's permission, I have brought you something for our marriage day, which I hope you will wear.'

He handed me a band box. I opened it and to my delight and surprise, found inside a beautiful new bonnet, adorned with cream ribbons. There was also a smaller package within. When I opened it, out fell the very cherry-coloured ribbons which I had coveted at Miss Greenwood's.

'My dear, thank you!' I cried, taking hold of his hand and fighting back tears. 'You are all kindness and I will do my very best to make you a good wife.'

'My love, it will be my life's work to make you happy!' replied he, also overcome with emotion.

We sat quietly together, our hands clasped, as the clock ticked away the hours towards our marriage day.

Sally

Sally is mentioned only once in the novel, in Chapter 47. As Elizabeth reads Lydia's note to Mrs Forster, written just before she eloped with Wickham, she is horrified at its levity. Having broken the news of her flight, revealed her love for Wickham, anticipated what a good joke it will be for her family to realise she is married, and apologised to Pratt (one of the officers) for missing a dance, she then turns to more practical household matters. We presume that she has fled with only the clothes on her back and whatever she can carry, but her mind is very much on her wardrobe. '... I wish you would tell Sally to mend a great slit in my worked muslin gown, before they are all packed up.' Elizabeth never believes that Wickham intended to marry her sister, but Lydia herself is planning ahead for her entry into Longbourn as a married woman, and the embroidered muslin dress clinging to her figure would have emphasised her new status. I wondered what Sally thought, being told to mend a frock belonging to a girl who had lost her character. I decided to make her a native of Hertfordshire, from a large working-class family used to unrelenting labour and being in service. Seeing Lydia, Mrs Forster and the other young girls through a servant's eyes gave me the chance to explore character and the nature of friendship in this story and I very much enjoyed researching Hertfordshire dialect and geography, as you'll see from all the footnotes.

FOR A POOR GIRL from Kimpton in the county of Hertfordshire, I have travelled further than ever I could have dreamed. Before John went for a soldier and Martha was wed, there was so many of us in our little cottage. The Colonel's lodgings in Brighton are bigger by far and there is only master, mistress, Mrs Taylor, Becky and me to fill the whole place up.

Father works for the squire up at the Hoo[6] and little brother George will follow him when he is old enough. I went into service at the big house when I was thirteen. I'm small, but I'm strong. We girls have helped mother bake bread, churn butter, do the wash, feed the stock, dig the garden and scour the pots since we were old enough to be trusted. What with Martha, John, Matilda, me, Jemima and George, and our little Annie too before the fever carried her

---

[6] Kimpton Hoo, a grand house built in the mid-seventeenth century with grounds landscaped and designed by Capability Brown in around 1762. A large, square, brick mansion with ivy on the walls and around 250 acres of park and farmland, it would have been the major employer for the surrounding villages. Kimpton village itself, where Sally and her family live, is seven miles north of St Albans. While Meryton is fictional, I have put references to real Hertfordshire locations throughout Sally's story. Kimpton Hoo was demolished in 1958 and much of the estate returned to agricultural use.

off two summers since, I wonder how we all fitted into our little cottage.

Martha went into service first. She ended up as the dairy maid at the Hoo. Sister Matilda followed her a year later, starting out as the scullery maid. It's cruel hard work. She'd come home crying with tiredness and mother would let her dip her hands in the big pot of goose grease to try to ease the cuts and sore places on her hands before she started again the next day. John worked on the farm with Father but it never suited him. He always fancied a more adventurous life than tilling the soil and digging parsnips so he married Brown Bess[7] and has been in the army these three Easters since.

I worked in the kitchens at the big house. I would rise from my bed while it was still dark, get dressed and take the pot downstairs to empty into the ditch beyond the vegetable patch. I shared a room with Martha and Matilda. They were up at the same time as me, but I'm the youngest, so I took out the slops. In the early morning while it was still dark, I would walk from our cottage up to the house with its walls covered in ivy and its many chimneys puffing smoke. It took a deal of wood and coal to keep the Hoo even tolerably warm while down in the kitchens, we were all sweating and red-faced with the heavy lifting and steam and the new-fangled open range roaring away fit to melt the bars.

---

[7] An eighteenth century term for joining the Army

A GREAT DEAL OF INGENUITY

†

At the big house, I got all the dirtiest jobs. Scouring the pots and pans in the scullery, washing down the floors, cooking up lye[8], ashes and lard for the soap, fetching the water and heating it up in the big copper, trying to stay out of the way of Mrs Mills, the cook, who had a nasty temper if ever I saw one. I worked there for two years before I rose to kitchen maid. My little sister Jemima came up to the big house to work as the scullery maid and Mother got the goose grease out again.

If you caught Mrs Mills in a good mood, she'd shew you how to make all the dainties the family liked to eat. Lemon tarts, possets, tea breads, almond cake, sponge fingers, currant bread – there was no end to what they would guzzle down every day. I was always hungry. You'd be dismissed without a character[9] if you were caught picking and stealing, so we knew better than to help ourselves.

One day, we were all in an uproar as the mistress had her eldest daughter's intended and his entire family coming to stay. The bells were ringing, Mrs Mills was purple in the face and giving anyone who stopped for a minute a good clout round the ear. 'Sally!' she yelled all of a sudden. 'Come here and make the pastry for the tarts! I've got all these raised pies to finish and Mistress ringing her bell every two minutes.'

---

[8] Lye, or sodium hydroxide, was commonly mixed with animal fat in the eighteenth century to make soap. The working classes would have made do with very harsh soap, but wealthier people used soap with lavender, honey, rose petals and other sweet smelling ingredients added for their delicate skin.
[9] Sacked without a reference

Mother always said I had a good hand with pastry. With bread, you need to thump and knead it around no end but pastry needs a cool hand and a quick touch. I went to work and got it made and into the pantry before Mrs Mills had finished her pie filling.

By the time we'd cleared away the dinner things, washed them and raked the coals over for the morning, we were fit to drop. I got back home too tired nearly to eat the supper Mother had made for me. I nearly fell over Martha and her intended cuddling in the porch. When she got married the next week, we walked up to the church, saw them wed and came home again to get on with the work. We miss her cheerful face and willing hands at home, but she's happily settled and expecting her first babe. I shouldn't think poor sister Matilda will ever find a man with her fainting fits and her twitch, and I have resolved that I will never marry. Mother will have to look to Martha and Jemima for the grandchildren.

Once old Mother Mills found I could make pastry as well as her, I got less clouts round the ear and more chance to cook. Soon, I could make a hot water crust as well as anyone. I was even trusted to make the mince pies.

†

Sister Jemima is friendly with the maids up at the big house. They're all local girls. She says the eldest girl's intended is a very handsome gentleman, but quick with his hands and always ready to give the young maids a handful of coins for services rendered. She whispered in my ear so that Mother would not hear. 'I'll be glad when they are married and he is away in Bedfordshire with her. No girl is safe with him around!' We giggled at the thought of being in Bedfordshire with a gentleman who cannot keep his breeches buttoned but stopped quickly when we saw Mother's eye upon us.

Miss Isabella, the mistress' eldest, is nearly one and twenty. She is a handsome young lady, but Jemima says that the talk of the staff is that she is too old for her husband. He likes very young ladies, the younger the better, and they say that he is marrying her only for her fortune, which is twenty thousand pounds. I have never seen three sovereigns together in one place, so cannot imagine how much money that might be. Enough for him to tie himself to a woman he does not care for, evidently.

With all the lace, and the bonnets and gowns, and the carriages and suchlike, Miss Isabella will have to keep her eyes shut and her head turned away if she is to have any happiness with her new husband. I should not like to think that my man was dipping his hands in the goose grease while my back was turned! Not that I would entertain the notion of encouraging one.

†

The year I turned seventeen, the militia came to Meryton, two miles from us in Kimpton. Mother warned all us girls to stay away from the soldiers. They'd ruin a poor girl soon as look at her and we none of us wanted to visit Mother Abigail in her little cottage in Kimpton Bottom. She'd take a penny to rid you of your trouble, but some girls died of the roaring fever a couple of days later. My friend Polly was one of them. She was going with the oldest Cox boy from Kimpton Mill, got into trouble and was dead and buried before she was seventeen.

I'd learnt all I could from Mrs Mills and I was ready to go on somewhere else. The Colonel of the regiment was looking for a steady girl to help the cook and housekeeper in his rented lodgings in Meryton. I started there in the April and from then on, I had only my own chamber pot to empty and a room all to myself.

†

I worked under Mrs Taylor, the Colonel's housekeeper and cook. She was a different kettle of fish to old Mother Mills. She didn't smell of stout, for a start, and she had a funny way of talking. She would call me, 'my duck' and 'hen.' She'd worked for the Colonel for years.

The Colonel's uniforms had to be kept clean, and his boots polished, and a good breakfast got ready bright and early. Once he had gone to the barracks, Mrs Taylor and I were left to ourselves to get on with the cleaning and scrubbing and cooking. Evening times, there would be company and we would be kept busy with keeping the gentlemen supplied with their drinks and suchlike. Servants work hard and keep their thoughts to themselves, but I felt that I had fallen on my feet with the Colonel. He paid us every quarter day[10] and gave no trouble.

✝

I'd been in Meryton for nigh on seven months when we first got wind of changes. The Colonel was often away from home, on business in Ware fourteen miles away, but he came back each time absent-minded and different, somehow. Mrs Taylor suspected there was a woman involved. 'Some sour-faced old widow, my duck, and that's the end of our comfy life,' she said one afternoon as we were making the pies for supper. 'Once the wife comes in the front door, the servants are worked to death.' I was grieved when she said this, and cried myself to sleep that night in my little attic room. I thought about looking for another situation, but as things turned out, I am pleased I did not.

November and December passed away as usual, with more work for us keeping the Colonel's uniforms clean with all the dirt and mud. He was away several times before Christmas, and all Mrs Taylor's fears were realised when he told us that he was to marry a Miss Richardson in January. 'Not a widow, hen,' sighed Mrs Taylor as we polished the Colonel's boots and sponged his breeches. 'Some pert little miss ringing her bell every five minutes and running us ragged.'

---

[10] In most of the UK in the eighteenth century, quarter days were the times when new servants were hired, school terms began and rents were due. They fell on four religious festivals, close to the two equinoxes and solstices and were traditionally 25th March, 24th June, 29th September and 25th December.

We got through Christmas, busy with card parties and suppers. The Colonel gave Mrs Taylor three new caps and me a dress length, which was good of him. Not that I had the time to make it up to wear and I have not the patience for needlework. Mrs Taylor said she would do it for me if I took over the soap making.

In the second week of January, the Colonel went to be married and on a cold and snowy winter's day, we waited for the sound of the carriage which would bring the new mistress home. We polished all the furniture, swept the floor with the tea leaves[11], beat the rugs, lit the fires and candles and made a supper to welcome them home.

†

I waited on table that evening in a clean cap and apron and I was surprized to see that the new mistress was no older than me. She was no beauty, but she had a sweet face that put me in mind of sister Martha. Her hair was the colour of corn and she smiled as I came in to the dining room. I went to my bed that night so tired I was asleep before my head was upon the pillow.

Having a new mistress gave us a deal more work. There was all the extra laundry and the rags[12] to soak and scrub every month. 'That will all be done within a few months, my duck,' Mrs Taylor said to me one day as the bread was

---

[11] Maids in the Regency period had to battle against dust and soot every day. To prevent dust flying up into the air and returning to its original place after cleaning, they would sprinkle wet, used tea leaves on the floor to trap the dust, then sweep them up.

[12] Sanitary protection.

rising. 'Then it will be stinking napkins[13] until the babe is breeched[14] and a new little one to see to, like as not.'

I could still remember the stink of filthy napkins soaking outside the kitchen at home. We were soaking, scraping, scrubbing and trying to get them clean until our fingers were raw. The mistress was young and healthy and would be breeding before too long. In the meantime, we were kept busy from morning to night, washing, drying, cooking, cleaning, serving, mending. The Colonel had always entertained the officers, but as a married man, he gave more suppers and card parties than ever before. The mistress soon made friends and her lodgings were full of giggling misses from noon to night. Mrs Taylor and I were constantly at the sugar loaf[15], making all the sweet dainties they called for. I was glad of my training at the Hoo under old Mother Mills.

There was a deal more washing, what with the mistress's shifts, nightgowns, frocks and furbelows[16]. My fingers were red and burning from scrubbing at the laundry. I cooked up the lye soap, adding ashes and lard to it and let it bubble on the fire. Such a stinking mess would not do for our master and his lady, so I added honey and lavender to it to make it fit for their delicate skin. No such luxuries for us – we washed under the freezing cold water from the pump in the yard using rough, hard soap. With such a small household, we were both up and down stairs constantly,

---

[13] Nappies.

[14] Taken out of nappies.

[15] Until the Late Victorian period, sugar was sold in a conical loaf and servants and cooks would take pieces off it for cooking and baking with specially designed sugar nips (large pincers with sharp blades).

[16] The pleated border of a petticoat or skirt.

and we had to put on clean aprons and caps when the bell rang so that we did not look like a pair of frights.

†

After two months of this, Mrs Taylor and I were worn out. Wash day stretched out for half the week and we would fall into our beds well after midnight every night, only to be up again at five, earlier on wash day to put the copper on. I am young and strong, well used to hard work, but poor Mrs Taylor began to suffer with dizzy spells and palpitations. One morning, just as we were heating the water to scour the pots after breakfast, she clapped her hand to her head and fell in a dead faint to the floor. I knew what to do. Sister Matilda suffers with the fits and would often measure her length on the kitchen floor at home.

As I was trying to bring Mrs Taylor round, the bell rang for the drawing room. My apron was greasy and dirty, my cap limp and my hands bright red from the cold water and rough soap. I could not leave Mrs Taylor, but the bell rang again. The poor woman started to sigh and her eyelids flickered, so I put a bundle of the Colonel's dirty linen under her head, praying that the smell would bring her round before I got back downstairs[17].

In the time it took me to change my apron and cap and tidy my hair, the bell had rung again. I ran upstairs and presented myself to Mrs Forster. 'Did not you hear me ring, Sally?" she asked, frowning a little and putting her head on

---

[17] Sally is using the Colonel's underwear to prop Mrs Taylor's head up. One can only imagine what a day of hard riding, marching and exercises would do to a gentleman's undergarments.

one side. "I am expecting Miss Kitty and Miss Lydia Bennet and the Harrington girls directly and I will need tea and some sponge cake sent up.'

I curtsied. 'Very good, ma'am. Right away, ma'am.' I hesitated. Even now, poor Mrs Taylor could be lying dead on the kitchen floor and the plates not even washed. 'Begging your pardon, ma'am, but Mrs Taylor is took bad. She had a turn while we were scouring the pots.'

Mrs Forster jumped up. To my amazement, she ran to the door and hurried down the stairs to the kitchen. For a fine lady, she was very light on her feet.

We descended into the kitchen. I was ashamed that the mistress should see the pots in soak and all the dirty linen in a heap on the floor. She walked straight past it and over to Mrs Taylor. Bless me if she didn't kneel down on the rough stone floor in her pretty dress and start chafing the poor woman's temples and wrists and talking to her in a quiet voice.

Presently, I heard the front door bell ring. 'Get that, please, Sally,' directed the mistress, by now gently dabbing poor Mrs Taylor's forehead with her own handkerchief, soaked in cool water. 'Tell the young ladies to wait in the drawing room.'

I ran back up the stairs and opened the door. There were the two Miss Bennets and the Harrington sisters. I could hear their silly giggling and shrieks halfway down the hall. Mother would have given any of us girls a clout round the ear if we'd been half as cheeky and pert.

In they all tumbled, and we spent several minutes in the hall while I hung up their spencers[18], scarves and bonnets. I shewed them into the drawing room and told them that Mrs Forster would be with them directly. Running back down to the kitchen, I was relieved to hear Mrs Taylor's voice and Mrs Forster's higher one rising up the stairs to meet me.

†

After Mrs Taylor's fainting fit, Mrs Forster spoke to her husband and we got a little workhouse brat by the name of Becky Scripps. She was a stunted little thing with huge staring eyes like a leveret dug out of its nest by a hungry fox. She slept on a pallet in my attic room and made no more noise than a mouse.

With Becky in the kitchen, the work eased. She could do plenty of the hard jobs, but she could have been no more than eleven or twelve and being half-starved and thin, she did not have the strength to lift heavy pots or carry the buckets of coal. Mrs Taylor made sure of her having enough to eat and after a while, her cheeks started to get some colour in them and she stopped twitching every time we spoke to her. Her arms were black and blue when she first came to us. Someone had been treating her rough, but she'd learned to work hard and not complain. With Mrs Taylor's good cooking and no more beatings, she was soon filling out a bit and getting stronger.

---

[18] A short, fitted jacket worn over a lady's gown

Mrs Forster was still entertaining her giggling friends every day which put a deal more work our way. No sooner had I baked up one lot of sponge cake than the bell would be ringing for more. What with the cooking and baking, and helping mistress with her hair and dressing in the morning, and the mending, I was run clean off my feet.

†

One morning, I had just finished washing all the pots and dishes with Becky while Mrs Taylor hung out the linen to bleach when we heard a ringing at the front door. I put on my clean apron and ran up the stairs. There stood the elder Miss Harrington, all by herself with a paper in her hand. 'Good day, Sally,' says she, walking in with her dusty shoes. 'Is Mrs Forster at home? I've brought her a sweet pattern for a gown.'

I shewed her into the drawing room where mistress was sitting and left them to their chatter. I knew well enough that they'd be calling for tea and sponge cake just as I got busy in the kitchen, but the bell staid silent which gave me time to get on with the dinner. I got Becky to peeling the potatoes while I started on the possets. Master was entertaining tonight which meant double the work.

Young Becky is a quick little thing. We've taken to sending her down to the butcher and the apothecary when something is needed and she notices everything that goes on in Meryton. I suppose that after years cooped up in the workhouse, a bit of fresh air and some new faces must be a right old treat for her.

'Those friends of mistress are running after the soldiers up and down the street,' she said. 'That Miss Lydia is the worst of the lot. She wouldn't last a minute in the workhouse. They beat the girls who came in with babes and no husband. Screaming and yelling and blood everywhere.' She shook her head as she scraped away at the potatoes.

I'd seen Miss Lydia's sort before. When I first went into service up at the big house, the mistress's youngest was exactly like her. She was the baby of the family and could do no wrong. Pert, silly, half-witted, she caused more work than the rest of them put together.

'She might flirt with half the militia, but she won't get herself landed with a brat,' I said, grating lemons for the possets. The juice soaked into the raw places on my hands and stung cruelly. 'Young ladies like her can do what they please until they find a husband, then all that's left is to breed and get fat for the rest of their lives.'

'I don't know as much.' Becky had finished the potatoes and was getting on with chopping the meat up. 'There was a girl in the workhouse used to have more food than the rest of us, and no beatings neither. She was the master's favourite, but the matron hated her. That girl had the same look in her eye as Miss Lydia. The master would go off with her while the rest of us worked and she'd come back smiling when all the work was done.'

It was a wicked shame that the mistress had taken up with such a clutch of gossipy misses. Meryton was full of them and they all seemed to end up in our drawing room making work for the kitchen. Miss Harrington was the best of them, not so loud and so silly as all the rest, although silly enough. She and the mistress seemed to be spending more time together for a mercy. The less we saw of Miss Lydia Bennet, the better.

†

At the end of April, the Colonel announced we were to quit Hertfordshire as the regiment was going down to Brighton for the summer. Mrs Taylor was as calm as you like about it, having moved around the country with the master for nigh on twenty years. 'One place is very like another, my duck,' she said comfortably, as we sat down to our supper. 'A nice bit of fresh sea air will put the roses into your cheeks, not that we'll be putting our noses outside the kitchen door.'

I'd never seen the sea. The furthest I'd been from Kimpton was Meryton, and that was barely two miles. It was nothing to young Becky who seemed not to care where she lived. I had no say in the matter, so I got on with packing up mistress' things and giving the lodgings a good scrubbing. One mercy was that the Colonel and mistress were going out nigh on every night to bid farewell to Meryton society, so there were fewer suppers to cook for. We had six weeks to pack everything up and get ourselves ready to move down to Brighton at the end of May, and for a mercy, it was fine sunny weather, good for drying and bleaching the linen and clothes.

†

Mother always used to say, 'Hertfordshire born, Hertfordshire bred, strong in the arm, but weak in the 'ead.'

She was right too. Saving father, and sister Martha's man, I never yet saw one of them I would give the time of day, let alone what poor Poll gave John Cox. Mother schooled us to work hard and keep ourselves decent. I was learning about baking, cooking and being a lady's maid. I could dress the mistress's hair to her satisfaction (not that she asked for much), do a bit of sewing although I hated it and keep her gowns fresh. I was already looking on to my next situation.

I wanted to move out of the kitchen and upstairs to a fine lady's dressing room. I would be sad to leave Mrs Taylor, and even young Becky, but in a year or two, I reckoned I'd be ready to go. I knew the mistress would give me a good character and I could earn a bit more too and let my poor hands heal from all the scrubbing.

I had my rags in to soak one morning in early May when Mrs Taylor started hanging out the linen to bleach in the spring sunshine. 'Mark my words, Sal,' she said as she pegged them over the line. 'Mistress is expecting. When did you last see her rags?'

I tried to think back. I knew I'd had them in the February because there was ice and snow on the ground and it was nigh on impossible to get hers and mine dried. Now I came to think about it, it had been a couple of months but I hadn't noticed with all the cooking and baking and running up and down stairs. That meant she would be having the babe around November with all the sunshine and good drying weather just a memory. A few months free of scrubbing the rags, then a couple of years of stinking napkins until the little one was breeched. I sighed. 'Better make sure we've laid in some goose grease, then.'

A GREAT DEAL OF INGENUITY

†

One afternoon, we were ironing and baking down in the kitchen. I was sprinkling lavender water on the mistress' gowns and the smell took me right back to home and mother doing the same thing. Becky was mixing up a sponge cake for me and Mrs Taylor was having five minutes with her feet up. Suddenly, the front door bell rang. It was Miss Lydia, as pert as you like. 'Good afternoon, Sally,' says she. 'Fine day, is not it?'

She untied her bonnet, handed it to me and skipped into the drawing room without a by-your-leave. I walked in behind her to see mistress sitting by herself with a letter in her hand. Her eyes were red, but she looked up and smiled at her visitor who was too wrapped up in herself to notice the traces of tears on her cheeks. 'Would you bring up tea, Sally, presently?' she asked. She never spoke to me as though I was beneath her, I'll give her that.

'And cake, Sally, some of that sponge cake,' interrupted Miss Lydia rudely. 'And lemon tarts if you've made any. Lord, I'm starving!'

She giggled and gave me a cheeky look. My hand tingled to box her ears and walk out, back to mother's, but a servant doesn't have the luxury of feelings. I curtsied. 'Yes, miss. Straight away, miss.'

Back down in the kitchen, I gave vent. 'Cheeky little piece! Who does she think she is?' I banged the plates down on the tray and started putting out sponge cake and the last of the lemon tarts which I'd wanted to serve later on after dinner. That meant more pastry making and grating up more lemons. At least once we were in Brighton, we wouldn't be seeing any more of Miss Lydia and her gaggle of half-witted friends.

I could hear shrieking and screeching coming from the drawing room as I walked up the hall with the tea and cake. Miss Lydia was capering about the room like a mad thing. 'I am to go to Brighton! Kitty will be wild! Oh, Harriet, I can hardly wait to tell Mama and get new clothes.'

My heart sank into my boots. What was the mistress thinking asking such an empty-headed little flirt to come with us to Brighton? Down in the kitchen, Mrs Taylor and I talked it over as I grimly grated more lemons for the tarts. More rags, more gowns, more linen, more shifts, more noise. We'd need a deal of sea air to make up for all that!

†

September in Brighton, and mistress' belly is swollen and her face pale as milk. Her sickness has stopped, which is a mercy and she eats next to nothing except bread and cheese. She barely goes out, what with her condition and the scandal. I don't know how long it will be before Miss Lydia's behaviour is forgot, and the part the Colonel and his lady played in it. Mrs Taylor and I knew the bold little flirt was no better than she should be, and when we had her washing to do, there it was, plain as day. She'd given that bit of red[19] license to have his way with her long before they ran off to London. Mrs Taylor wrinkled her nose as she plunged her linen into the water and lye. 'Smoke, ale and

---

[19] Soldier.

something that'll swell her stomach before too long. She'll have the French disease[20] before six months are gone by.'

Poor mistress. She puts on a brave face, but it's a shame the way she was treated. Master did his best, riding all the way back to Hertfordshire to talk to Miss Lydia's family. I hear she's married to the gentleman now, a Mr Wickham Mrs Taylor says, and much good may it do her.

The last piece of work I ever did for the ungrateful little chit was to mend her precious worked muslin gown. She had torn it right across the skirt and had the cheek to write to the mistress asking her to ask me to stitch it up for her. I had no choice, but I cursed her with every stab of the needle.

†

Mrs Taylor was right. One place is very much like another. The scream of the sea-gulls swooping over the lodgings reminds me of the noise of Miss Lydia and her friends in the drawing room. The tang of the sea in the air takes me back to pig-killing time at home when the beast was salted down for winter. The crash of the waves on the beach puts me in mind of Father's gun as he shot the rooks for pies. Brighton is noisy and dirty and full of dangers as far as I can see, and I know no-one save Mrs Taylor, Becky and the master and mistress. On the rare occasions I venture out on to the dusty streets, I keep my eyes down and myself to

---

[20] Syphilis. Interestingly, the French called it, "the English disease". Sufferers could expect to experience fatigue, weight loss, headaches, swollen lymph nodes and, as it wore on, brain damage and muscle paralysis. Pregnant women could also pass it to their unborn child.

myself. There are plenty of red coats to be seen and the laughter of fine young ladies in their muslin gowns. All I can think of is the shame brought upon my mistress' house by that untamed little flirt, Mrs Wickham as we must now call her.

I will not leave the Forsters to go and be a lady's maid. Better the stench of a baby's napkins and the bubbling pot of lye than what we saw on Miss Lydia's gowns and linen. As mother always used to say, 'A careless girl is a side pocket for a toad[21].' Mrs Taylor, not being from Hertfordshire, didn't get my meaning, but when I explained, she nodded and sighed.

'Well, well, my duck, talking won't get dinner on the table. Becky, hen, wipe the plates down, Sal, let's get those potatoes in the tureen and I'll get the wine out of the cellar. They'll be ringing the bell for dinner before we know where we are.'

---

[21] The modern equivalent would be "As much use as a chocolate teapot".

The Reverend Mr Annesley

Mrs Annesley is part of Mr Darcy's household both in London and Derbyshire, acting as his sister's companion. Although she is never given any dialogue in the novel, we can glean quite a lot of information about her from other characters' observations. A companion was not regarded as a servant, but she was certainly not equal in class to her employer. Traditionally, companions were respectable middle-class women who had no other means of supporting themselves. The role involved providing improving company and conversation a young unmarried girl, supporting her as she entertained guests and learned to perform the role of a hostess and accompanying her to social events, such as dances and balls. She also acted as a chaperone, vital for a young unmarried girl of good birth. The companion had comfortable accommodation in the family part of the house (certainly not in the servants' quarters), she would eat with the family and be paid a small salary. No heavy lifting for these ladies – the hardest work they had to do was some embroidery, light mending, pouring out tea and giving instructions to the servants. We first meet her in Chapter 45, when Elizabeth and the Gardiners pay a formal visit to Miss

Darcy, Mrs Hurst and Miss Bingley at Pemberley. As you would expect, the latter two ladies are barely civil, and there is an awkward silence. However, Georgiana's companion knows the social ropes and saves the day. 'By Mrs Hurst and Miss Bingley, they were noticed only by a curtsey; and on their being seated, a pause, awkward as such pauses always must be, succeeded for a few minutes. It was first broken by Mrs Annesley, a genteel, agreeable-looking woman, whose endeavour to introduce some kind of discourse, proved her to be more truly well-bred than either of the others; and between her and Mrs Gardiner, with occasional help from Elizabeth, the conversation was carried on.' She is mentioned one more time in Chapter 54 when Mr Darcy tells Elizabeth his sister is now alone at Pemberley with her, the Bingleys and Hursts having finally left. Mrs Annesley began to take shape in my head, a respectable clergyman's widow with a great fondness for her husband's sermons. Certainly a woman ideally placed to watch the power play and dynamics between her employer and the various ladies who pass through his household.

MY DEAR HUSBAND, Rector of Osgathorpe in the County of Leicestershire was always able to soothe my ruffled nerves by saying:

'Louisa my dear, remember that a wise man will hear, and will increase learning; and a man of understanding shall attain unto wise counsels[22].'

Even now, since I had the great misfortune to lose him three winters since, his words and wise counsels still echo in my memory. Whenever I am vexed, or require advice, I look into his sermons, which he had printed and bound at his own expence, and which would make most improving reading for all young persons who wish to tread the narrow path of righteousness. What joy and right-thinking pride would mount in my breast as I sat in our pew listening to his discourse on a Sunday morning. But I forget myself. I am no longer the rector's wife, mistress of my own household. I am plain Mrs Annesley, companion to Miss Georgiana Darcy, of Grosvenor Square and Pemberley in the county of Derbyshire.

In my nightly prayers, I give grateful thanks to our Lord for supplying all my wants in such a providential fashion. My dear husband left me moderately well provided for, but I did not have enough to live extravagantly. (Not that I would wish to! A modest and economical life glorifies the Lord.)

†

Since last autumn, I have been employed as companion to Miss Darcy. This past year has been one of the happiest I have known since losing my dear husband. Miss Darcy is a sweet, gentle young lady. She is but sixteen years old and

---

[22] Proverbs 1:5, King James Version

has not been used to society. We are presently come from her establishment in Grosvenor Square up to Pemberley, the home of Miss Darcy's brother, Mr Fitzwilliam Darcy.

I believe that the Darcys are one of the first families in England, yet Miss Darcy and her brother exhibit no improper pride. As the daughter and widow of a clergyman, I am always watchful for sinful vaingloriousness and ungodly behaviour, and I have found neither in the Darcy family. Miss Darcy keeps her prayer book by her bed and is most faithful in church attendance. Her brother is charitable to the poor, and a good and attentive landlord. I am minded of my dear husband's sermon on the Parable of the Tenants[23], but even with a good stock of beeswax candles provided by my munificent employer, I cannot risk straining my eyes before dinner by reading even the first lines, since my husband had a great deal to say on the subject.

†

Having spent my youth in peripatetic fashion, moving from parish to parish with my dear father and mother, we came finally to rest in the village of Breedon on the Hill, with its fine old church. This was my father's last parish, and had the good Lord not moved him to settle there, my life would have been very different.

I taught the children of the village on a Sunday and found that I had a natural turn for instruction. With no fortune and no beauty to speak of, I knew that I would have

---

[23] Matthew 21: 33-46 from the Authorised (King James) Version of the Bible

to make my own way in the world. For several years, I taught the children in the village and soon I was instructing them in such letters, figuring and reading as it was their status to learn. I loved my little scholars and to know that I was doing the Lord's work filled me with joy. I went on in this way until I was two and twenty when my dear father was taken to be with his Maker and my mother and I were cast upon the charity of her older brother and his family.

We packed up our small belongings and said good-bye to our home with many tears. We travelled by post chaise to my uncle's home in Alvaston, over the Leicestershire border to Derbyshire. It was not sixty miles from our home, but as the chaise clattered into the village, it seemed another and a sadder world.

†

My aunt had five children when first we came to Alvaston, and four more were born during our time there. I was kept busy helping her with the older ones and soon it became clear that I could earn my keep by teaching them. This I did with pleasure, and while my aunt and my dear mother were occupied with the younger ones, I found myself teaching my neices and nephews reading, writing and arithmetic. They were dear, sweet children, although boisterous.

My aunt and uncle attended church with us every Sunday, but we were sad to note that they merely observed the proprieties and lived mainly for the world. I prayed nightly that they would come to a deeper understanding of our Lord and His many mercies, but it seemed unlikely as my aunt focused chiefly on visiting, gossip and new clothes.

Still, my dear mother and I were most grateful for their kindness in giving us a home.

†

Life continued without incident until the Easter of my eight and twentieth year. On Easter Sunday, we walked to church as usual and I noticed that there was an unfamiliar gentleman sitting in the front pew. He looked to be a clergyman, as he was clothed in black habiliments[24] and had a respectable and serious countenance. After the service was over, the rector introduced him to us as his nephew, Mr George Annesley.

The next Sunday, after the service was over, Mr Annesley approached me in the porch. We spoke for some time and by the end of our conversation, he had skilfully drawn from me the reason for our living in Alveston, our history and my enjoyment of teaching little children. In turn, I had learned that he held the living of Stanton by Dale, some five and sixty miles to the north. I observed my mother and aunt in conversation outside and shortly afterwards, my aunt approached Mr Annesley and invited him to supper.

Thus began our short courtship. By Michaelmas, I was married to Mr Annesley and living in Stanton by Dale.

---

[24] Clothes worn for a particular purpose or profession, in this case, that of a clergyman in the Church of England.

A GREAT DEAL OF INGENUITY

✝

My married life was a harmonious one. My husband was a kindly and generous man, with a deep knowledge of the Scriptures and a most engrossing manner of preaching. Sundays were a particular joy for me, now a respectable married woman with my own household and the opportunity to teach the children on a Sunday afternoon. My only sadness was the parting from my dear mother. We wrote often, but five and sixty miles is too far to travel for a clergyman's wife absorbed in her duties, and I sometimes shed a quiet tear when my husband was locked up in his study writing his Sunday sermon.

My other, private grief was that we had no living children of our own to cheer and bless us. Our little boy lived only for one night and one day then was taken from us. I know we will meet again in Heaven, but it was many, many months until I could be reconciled to the loss of my little one. Even now, a widow in my six and fiftieth year, I still recall the tiny flutterings like the brush of birds' wings, the proud swell of my stomach and the weight of his velvety head in the crook of my arm.

✝

Life continued with my husband and all my parish duties. As a childless wife, I had no little dependants to take up my time at home, so I was able to visit the poor, the sick and the needy, assist my dear husband in his work and ensure that our home was always a welcoming and comforting place. My teaching continued to be a joy and a blessing to me. While I believed in firm discipline to keep children on the straight and narrow path which leads to salvation (a theme to which my husband returned time and again in his sermons), yet I was often reminded of our dear Lord's exhortation in the gospel of Matthew. 'Take heed that ye despise not one of these little ones; for I say unto you, That in heaven their angels do always behold the face of my Father which is in heaven[25].'

I confess that sometimes during the Sunday service I would allow my mind to wander and engage in idle fancies. My own lost little one I saw as a cherub frolicking and running in the courts of Heaven, just as he would have done in our garden at home.

For this reason, I believe, I taught my little charges with love and compassion, and was rewarded with their affection in return. Even now, in my comfortable sitting room looking out on to the wooded hills of the Pemberley estate, tears still sting my eyes as I recall my scholars' little hands which would slip into mine, the little lisping voices and the bright eyes.

†

We lived at Stanton by Dale for twelve years, until Mr Annesley was offered the living at Osgathorpe and I returned once again to my beloved Leicestershire.

I wept when we left Stanton. It held many happy memories of my early married days, it was the home of the

---

[25] Matthew 18:10, from the Authorised (King James) Version of the Bible

birth and death of my little baby, as well as the place where I had been blessed with the teaching of so many precious young souls. Many of those sweet children had been toddling when first I arrived, and were now almost ready to join their older brothers and sisters in service.

Some, to my great grief, had been taken to be with the Lord. My particular pet, Annie Steeples, carried off by fever, her brother Alfred two years later tumbling into the pond and drowning, Mary Spendlove dying of the bloody flux along with the two little Wheatcroft boys – I cannot write more, as my tears threaten to blur the ink.

†

We settled into our comfortable rectory at Osgathorpe and although I missed all my dear friends and the sweet children most painfully, I soon began to form attachments to our new parish. One of the greatest joys of living there was that I found myself not fifteen miles away from my dear mother at Alvaston. We kept a curricle and horses at Osgathorpe which meant I could venture further afield when my husband did not need our equipage for parish work. I found my mother sadly aged, but with her unquenchable spirit still very much in evidence. My aunt, too, had lost the vigour and elasticity of spirit I had always observed in her, and with her grey hair and trembling hands, I barely recognised the merry, high-spirited matron of former days.

How cruel is the passing of time! I was reminded of my dear husband's sermon on the first chapter of 1 Peter. 'For all flesh is as grass, and all the glory of man as the flower of grass. The grass withereth, and the flower thereof falleth away: but the word of the Lord endureth forever[26].'

My aunt and uncle had experienced the bitter loss of a child since we last met. Their eldest daughter, the mother of two little children, died bringing forth a third babe, who was also snatched up to Heaven. My poor aunt had a seizure when she heard the news and became afflicted with shaking hands and a nervous disposition. While once she lived for fine new clothes and gossip, now she wore black and rarely left the house.

Within a year of our move to Osgathorpe, my dear mother went to be with her Saviour, dying quietly in her bed. She left me my father's Bible and letters, as well as her ebony cross and jet earrings which I wear daily. My unfortunate aunt was not far behind, slipping away a few months later. With her death, the household was broken up, my uncle and his youngest children (the rest all being married and settled) moving to Derby.

†

My last and greatest loss came fourteen years after we moved to Osgathorpe. It was a bitter winter, with snow on the ground. A family of poor brickmakers living in a damp cottage by the River Soar was in need of food and medicine. I made nourishing soup and took physick[27] to them and brought back the sad news that the man of the house and two of his children were close to death. My dear husband,

---

[26] 1 Peter 1:24-25 from the Authorised (King James) Version of the Bible
[27] Medicine.

always burning with zeal to help others, galloped off on his horse to tend to their physical and spiritual needs. He returned later that night, cold, shivering and soaked through from the heavy snowflakes which had begun tumbling from the leaden skies shortly after his departure.

He now was the one in need of physick. The apothecary sent powders and draughts while I sat by his bedside praying and imploring the Lord to spare him. On the third night of watching and praying, my dear husband had a moment of clarity in his restless fever. I had fallen into a light doze and was awoken by his dear voice calling, 'Louisa!'

'Yes, my love,' I whispered, drawing near to the bed and clasping his hand in mine. His voice was hoarse and faint and I had to put my ear close to his mouth to hear him.

'I see him, Louisa. I see our dear little Thomas. He is waiting for me. I must go, for I am called, but I leave you to carry on our good work. Dearest Louisa!

He fell back on his pillows, wracked with coughing, his cheeks flushed and hectic and his eyes glittering with fever. I looked where his gaze was fixed, praying that I too would glimpse our beloved little son waiting at the gates of Heaven. I saw nothing and a few minutes later, my dear husband was no more.

†

I will pass quickly over the sad months of early widowhood which followed. Due to the kindness of Mrs Woods, the doctor's wife, I found myself living in a tiny cottage near the forge. My husband had left me tolerably comfortably off, but with neither chick nor child, I suffered great grief and a feeling of uselessness. I, who had been the vicar's daughter and the rector's wife, found myself now simply a lonely widow. I tried to carry on my husband's work, visiting the cottagers, helping the sick and needy and taking part in the life of the village, but the new rector and his family were in residence and I did not wish to be a nuisance to them. At four and fifty, it seemed that my useful life was over.

†

Summer came, but for the first time in my life, the blue skies, white clouds and fresh green mantles on the trees did not bring the customary rise in my spirits. Mrs Woods invited me to take tea with her one fine June morning. We sat in her pretty parlour looking out over the garden, alive with fragrant roses, stocks and hollyhocks. She looked into my face and took my hand.

'My dear Mrs Annesley, it grieves me to see you so wan and sad. I know the loss of a beloved husband is hard to bear, and for such a busy and useful person as yourself, this must be painful indeed.'

I was grateful for her kindness. Haltingly, and punctuated by many tears, I attempted to tell her of my feelings. There was a soft knock at the door and Mrs Woods' housemaid walked in. 'Begging your pardon, ma'am, the butcher's boy is at the back door.'

'Thank you, Mary. Excuse me, please, Mrs Annesley, I will return directly.' She walked briskly out of the room, leaving me to gaze at the beautiful summer garden, bees buzzing, birds swooping and crying and brightly coloured flowers everywhere. All seemed to be fertile and alive and full of hope.

I buried my face in my handkerchief and gave myself up to grief. Sitting in my widow's cap, I mourned afresh for my lost boy, that I would never see him take a wife and present me with grandchildren to love. I was still in this state when Mrs Woods walked back into the room.

She poured me a fresh cup of scalding hot tea and insisted that I drink it. It did me good. Drawing a letter from her pocket, Mrs Woods told me of her friend, Mrs Reynolds, the housekeeper at a great house in Derbyshire. They had been girls together in Matlock and kept up their correspondence throughout all their lives. 'Mrs Reynolds writes that a genteel, respectable woman is required to act as a companion to a young lady, living with her in her establishment in London and travelling with her to Pemberley, in Derbyshire when required. My dear, why do you not write and put yourself forward for the situation? There could be no-one kinder or more ladylike than yourself.'

I returned home to my little house, fell to my knees and asked God for guidance. I felt Him direct me to my dear husband's sermons. The folio fell open at one of his most affecting and learned discourses, preached on Genesis 12. The words of the first verse struck me and I wept afresh, thanking the Lord for his mighty provision. 'Now the Lord had said unto Abram, Get thee out of thy country, and from thy kindred, and from thy father's house, unto a land that I will shew thee…[28]' It had been many years since I had lived in my father's house, and my kindred were few, but I believed most fervently that it was time to turn my face from the past and to accept a new situation in life.

†

Never yet have I made a mis-step guided by the wise words of my late husband. I was offered and accepted the position of companion to Miss Darcy and so began a new chapter in my life. I moved from my little house in Osgathorpe to my new apartment at Pemberley in the middle of August last year. Mrs Woods proved herself a true friend, helping me to pack my trunks and making tea whenever I began to droop with fatigue.

Mr Darcy wishes that his sister should begin to take her place in society, although I believe that left to herself, the young lady would be perfectly happy playing the piano in her sitting room and never venturing out to meet any new acquaintance.

I am treated as a member of the household, well supplied with whatever I need. I have my own private sitting room and have been given the use of a little phaeton and ponies whenever I am not required by Miss Darcy. Her brother is a liberal and generous employer.

Mrs Reynolds and I have formed a most affectionate friendship. She is a sensible and agreeable woman, faithful in her Bible reading and a great support to me in my new life. We often drink tea together in my sitting room while

---

[28] Genesis 12:1, from the Authorized (King James) Version of the Bible.

looking out over the beautiful Derbyshire countryside. I miss her companionship most exceedingly when we return to Grosvenor Square, where the servants are respectful but light-hearted and giddy, and without the gravity and seriousness of manner which can only come from a strong Christian faith.

†

The family party is often augmented by friends and acquaintances and this summer was no exception. Mr Bingley (a close friend of Mr Darcy), his two sisters and the elder lady's husband travelled with us from London to Pemberley. I took at once to young Mr Bingley, a most pleasant and well-bred gentleman who was particularly solicitous in ensuring my comfort on the journey. I like to think that my little Thomas would have become such a man.

I could not conjure up such warm feelings towards the rest of the party. Mr Bingley's two sisters were very fine ladies indeed. They wore rich silks, a great deal of jewellery and did not have the friendly demeanour of their brother. Mr Hurst, the husband of the elder lady, could not seem to keep my name in his head and variously addressed me as, 'Mrs Ainsley', 'Mrs Annaby' and "Mrs Errrr.' As a Christian, I forgave him from my heart and spent much of the journey in quiet contemplation and prayer.

We arrived at Pemberley to find Mr Darcy already in residence. Miss Darcy ran to meet him, her countenance aglow. He greeted his other guests with great politeness, but it was clear to me that his sister was the person he longed to see above all others. Miss Bingley behaved in a most indecorous fashion, talking and laughing in an affected manner whenever Mr Darcy was near, and treating his house as though it was her own. It was not long before my instincts told me that she hoped to become Mrs Darcy before the year was out. A less suitable helpmeet for my young lady's brother could hardly be imagined. She attends church in her finest clothing, yawns openly during the sermon and once (so I observed) fell fast asleep during the homily. Such a person should not be the mistress of a great estate such as Pemberley. I have not spoken to Miss Darcy about it, for it would not be my place, but I believe that young as she is, she too feels the impropriety of Miss Bingley's behaviour.

†

Mr Hurst continues idle and ill-bred. It is plain that to him, I am no better than a servant and he treats me accordingly. The ladies are little better, although they do at least acknowledge me, albeit coldly and briefly. My dear young lady, however, is all sweetness and gentleness towards her visitors, and her brother a true gentleman. The day after we had arrived, we had hardly settled in when Miss Darcy came to tell me that she, her brother and Mr Bingley were taking the curricle to pay a visit to some acquaintances in nearby Lambton. I had some mending to do, so welcomed the opportunity to sit quietly in my sitting room enjoying the beautiful views from the windows. Before I picked up my needle, I fell to my knees (slowly, as my joints are stiff and painful with advancing age) and gave thanks once again to my Maker for His providential goodness to me.

Upon Miss Darcy's return, we put on our bonnets and took a turn under the spreading Spanish chestnuts and down to the river, a favourite walk of hers. She was more animated than ever I had seen her as she told me of her delight and pleasure in being introduced to an acquaintance of Mr Darcy and Mr Bingley, a Miss Elizabeth Bennet from Hertfordshire. I was glad indeed to hear of another young lady in her social circle, since I do not think that Mrs Hurst and Miss Bingley with their pert manners and snobbish behaviour are the kind of ladies to benefit her. I must hope and pray that Miss Bennet is a well-bred and devout young lady, who will prove to be a valuable friend to Miss Darcy.

That evening, as we took our coffee after dinner and waited for the gentlemen to join us after their port, Miss Bingley was more disagreeable than ever. I had constantly to remind myself of my dear husband's dictum, 'Louisa, judge not lest ye be judged[29]'. She was wholly disrespectful in her conversation, making remarks of a most unpleasant manner about Miss Bennet, who, I understand, is a slight acquaintance of hers from her time in Hertfordshire. Mrs Hurst, who, as a married woman, should have known better and taken her sister to task, joined in with every appearance of pleasure. Between them, they judged the poor young lady on every point of countenance, manners and class with many shrieks of laughter. Miss Darcy, well-

---

[29]Matthew 7:1, from the Authorized (King James) Version of the Bible.

bred and polite as always, took up her embroidery and ignored them.

When the gentlemen came in, Mr Hurst lay down on a sopha and went to sleep. It is not for a respectable Christian woman to notice such things, but my close proximity enabled me to see port stains on his waistcoat and that his breeches were in sore need of mending, as the seams were near splitting. Mr Hurst enjoys the good things of the table, I have observed.

†

Two days later, the visit was returned by Miss Bennet and her aunt Mrs Gardiner. The latter was most respectable-looking and pleasant, while the young lady was extremely pretty, with lovely dark eyes and a most charming manner. The difference between herself and Miss Bingley was marked. I was reminded of my dear late husband's discourse on 1 Peter:3 about the adornment of women. Miss Bennet was wearing a simple, but elegant costume and her face glowed with health. Miss Bingley, on the other hand, was bedizened with plumes, rustling silks and ornaments and her face fell as she walked into the saloon with her sister and saw us sitting there.

One of my roles with Miss Darcy is to gently encourage her to take up the duties a young lady of fortune and rank should bear. Her natural reticence makes this painful for her and I pity her for it. My young charge haltingly made the necessary introduction, and I quickly realised that I should have to draw upon my many years of parish experience to avoid an uncomfortable social situation. Mrs

Hurst and Miss Bingley did not speak, but merely made their curtseys before sitting down on a sopha. There was silence. They evidently did not intend to notice Miss Bennet and her aunt, while my young lady was too shy and inexperienced to begin a conversation. It therefore fell to me to begin, which I did by asking our visitors if they were pleased with Derbyshire.

A most agreeable conversation then commenced. Mrs Gardiner had spent her youth in the county and was enjoying the renewal of old friendships and acquaintances. She had the courtesy to ask me of my own connections and we were soon talking with great enjoyment of our past lives. Miss Darcy occasionally spoke in a very low voice, but then coloured and was silent. Miss Bennet, I observed, pitied her hostess for her shyness and addressed her several times in a kindly fashion. My prayers have been answered. We must hope that her travels bring her once more to Derbyshire and that she spends enough time in town with her aunt and uncle to become a valuable acquaintance for my young lady.

Mrs Hurst and Miss Bingley sat like two graven images on their sopha in the meantime, and I observed a shadow cross Miss Bingley's haughty features each time Miss Bennet spoke. I cannot imagine what offence such an amiable young lady could have committed to be treated so. I made sure to smile at Miss Bennet and encourage Miss Darcy to reply to her when addressed.

After a few moments had passed, the footmen, James and William, walked in with cold meat, some sponge cake (as light as a cloud) and a beautiful selection of fruits from the glass houses. The head gardener, Mr Castledine, grows produce the like of which I have never seen. Peaches, nectarines, grapes, cherries, apples, plums, medlars, pears and all the berries in season. On my walks around the grounds, he will often stop work to greet me and we speak of cultivation, varieties and our own particular favourites. My dear husband was very fond of fruit and I would work hard during the summer months by bottling and preserving it for the winter. Mr Castledine started as the gardener's boy at Pemberley in his youth, I understand, and is a most respectable and hard-working man.

But I digress. I gently encouraged Miss Darcy to take her post as hostess and Miss Bennet, Mrs Gardiner and myself continued our conversation. The gentlemen presently walked in and animation wreathed itself on Miss Bingley's countenance. My suspicions of her motives towards my employer were confirmed. I saw Mrs Gardiner's eyes turn briefly towards her with a look of surprize. The gentlemen were all politeness towards their guests and I could not help but see Miss Bingley's face change when Mr Darcy spoke to Miss Bennet. I feared that her heart was overtaken with jealousy, a terrible and besetting sin indeed.

As Miss Bennet finished her tea and replaced her cup in its saucer, Miss Bingley finally spoke directly to her in a cutting fashion.

'Pray, Miss Eliza, are not the militia removed from Meryton? They must be a great loss to your family.'

Miss Bennet's cheeks were mantled with a rising blush, but she remained composed and replied civilly. Miss Darcy, however, changed colour and clasped her hands tightly in her lap, her eyes downcast and her cheeks burning. Her brother's complexion likewise was heightened and he fixed his eyes on Miss Bennet's face. I knew not what to think and an involuntary glance at Mrs Gardiner shewed her equally confused.

Again, it fell to me to carry on the conversation which I did, talking most earnestly of the weather. Over the course of a long life, I have found that this is one topic on which everyone can discourse, at any time. Awkward pauses in social intercourse are not to be tolerated and the truly well-bred person will always find themselves able to encourage suitable conversation.

Presently, the ladies rose to leave and Mr Darcy accompanied them to their carriage. The moment he had left the room, Miss Bingley burst out with a torrent of ill-natured abuse against Miss Bennet. To her great credit, Miss Darcy refused to join her. I longed to absent myself, but could not while my charge remained in the saloon. On Mr Darcy's return, Miss Bingley (in a most unchristian fashion) repeated some of the comments she had been making about my employer's guest, criticising her complexion, her manners and her bearing in a sharp and shrewish manner. Pride cometh before a fall[30], and after a particularly unkind attack on Miss Bennet's looks, my employer silenced Miss Bingley with a few heart-felt sentences and left the room. We were left to our private thoughts, and for once I forgot my duty to encourage my young charge to play and sing or join in the conversation. I was busy conjecturing what the future might hold.

---

[30]Proverbs 16:18, from the Authorized (King James) Version of the Bible.

†

As I dressed for dinner, my mind was greatly occupied. I found a rapidly growing dislike for Mr Darcy's friends growing in my heart. I was in such a flutter of spirits that I buttoned up my sleeve wrong, twice, and completely forgot to look into my husband's sermons, which I generally do before dinner to compose myself.

As I was doing up my buttons for the third time, there was a soft tap at my door. Miss Darcy came in, smiling, as she always did. From my first day at Pemberley, we have always walked down to dinner together. Her sweet nature is a credit to her. I will never have a daughter or a granddaughter of my own but, had I been blessed with one, I could have wished that she was exactly like my young charge.

I invited her to take a seat while I finished dressing. I am become sensitive to her every mood, living in such close proximity every day, and I fancied I saw a cloud on her smooth young face. 'Does something trouble you, my dear?' I asked, adjusting my cap. Miss Darcy walked to the window and gazed out over the hills. I could see that her heart was full and it has been my experience that when young people wish to speak, we older folk should not discourage them by continually pressing them. I remained silent and waited until she was ready to talk of what troubled her.

'What was your impression of Miss Bennet and her aunt, Mrs Annesley?' she asked after a long pause, turning to face me.

'I found Mrs Gardiner a very well-bred and agreeable lady, my dear,' I replied, settling my shawl around my shoulders. 'Miss Bennet was most charming, with delightful manners and a very pretty way of speaking. I trust that they will be paying us another visit.'

Miss Darcy's face was all aglow. In company, she rarely smiles, but our close relationship has enabled me to see her true character, a warm, thinking and affectionate one.

'Oh, Mrs Annesley, I do hope that the acquaintance continues! Miss Bennet is so agreeable and engaging in her manners. I would like to know her better. She and her aunt are to drink tea with us on the morrow. She tells me she has four sisters at home. How I would have loved to have had a sister.'

'Did you not have friends of your own age at school, my dear?' I asked.

'Oh, yes, there were several very pleasant girls, but my closest friend was Miss Grantley. We were intimate friends, but she was taken from school a month before I and lives now with her family in Devonshire. It is such a long way away.' She sighed, and her face fell.

'We write often to each other, and I hoped that she might visit us in London, but her last letter told me of her engagement to a gentleman whose seat is in Lincolnshire, so it seems unlikely.'

My heart ached for her. While rich, comfortable and handsome, she did not seem to have enjoyed those close friendships which my observations have told me young people require. With only one much older brother and no parents, she lacked the society which other young ladies of her age enjoyed. Boldly, I mentioned our current company.

'You have been acquainted with Mrs Hurst and Miss Bingley for many years, have you not? They are older than you, but surely Mr Bingley's younger sisters would be suitable friends?'

I observed a number of emotions cross my young lady's countenance. 'I have known them since I was a child, but I was away at school for much of my life, and by the time I was old enough to form a closer friendship, Mrs Hurst was engaged and Miss Caroline Bingley was much involved with the preparations for the marriage. Miss Harriet and Miss Anne were at school and Miss Leonora a child of ten. I…' She hesitated, and I waited patiently until she felt able to speak once more.

'Mr and Mrs Hurst and Miss Bingley spend a great deal of time with Mr Bingley at his house in London, and therefore my brother is also often in their company. He wishes very much for me to become more used to society. For this reason, I believe, he has encouraged me to spend time with the Bingleys and Mr and Mrs Hurst.' She was silent again, her fingers twisting her handkerchief around and around. I did not press her, for it was plain to see that she felt uncomfortable.

The silence was broken by the sound of my little clock chiming the hour. I pride myself that I am never late for anything. Arm in arm, we walked downstairs to dinner.

†

We spoke no more of our company or of Miss Bennet and her aunt that evening. I could see, however, that my young lady had formed a great admiration for Miss Elizabeth and that Miss Bingley's unchristian and unkind remarks upon her were hurtful to her. I noted that Miss Bingley had ceased making them in Mr Darcy's presence, but her manners towards him were even more pert and unladylike than before. If he sat down to compose a letter, she would stand behind him, remarking on his handwriting. If he selected a volume from the shelf, she would begin to read the second volume, discoursing loudly and often upon her understanding of it. She continued to play cards and talk uncharitably of her wider acquaintance with her sister and Mr Hurst, while Mr Darcy was largely silent and thoughtful. Mr Bingley remained delightful, a charming and amiable young man with engaging manners. In his company, I noted, Miss Darcy was chattier and more at ease than with anyone else, excepting myself. Could it be…? But no, this was not for me to know.

†

At breakfast the next morning, I noted that nearly every member of the party appeared burdened with apprehension, anxiety and contemplation. The exception was Mr Hurst, who had changed his stained waistcoat and was bursting out of a clean pair of breeches. During my married life, morning prayers and afterwards breakfast was the happiest time of the day. We would sit looking out of our windows on to the garden discoursing in the most delightful fashion and giving thanks to our Lord for His munificent blessings. At Pemberley, however, breakfast was a largely silent meal.

This morning was no exception. Mr Hurst ate and drank, and drank and ate in a fashion which intruded painfully upon my thoughts. His consumption of grilled bone, chops, kidneys and buttered eggs was both gluttonous and noisy. His wife toyed with her cup of chocolate, while Miss Bingley's sharp eyes darted around the table, resting most often upon Mr Darcy who was silent and lost in thought. Mr Bingley alone seemed in good spirits and disposed to talk. Miss Darcy spoke only when spoken to.

'What plans have you today, Darcy?" asked Mr Bingley cheerfully. "It is a fine day for fishing.'

Mr Darcy looked up from his eggs. 'I am riding into Lambton after breakfast then I must call on old Bestwick at the home farm to see about his fences.'

Miss Bingley looked up, hope gleaming in her eyes. 'I long to ride out today. Lambton is charming and I would welcome the exercise. Louisa, what think you?'

Mrs Hurst shook her head.

'Lord, Caroline, the roads are thick with dirt and you would come back looking like our dear Miss Bennet with your petticoat quite six inches deep in dust, up to your ancles in dirt.'

Mr Darcy let out a noise between a snort and a sigh and pushed back his chair impatiently. 'Georgiana, I wish that you and Mrs Annesley would take a turn in the grounds. The weather is fine but will break before long. It will be injurious to your health to remain indoors on such a fine day.'

He walked quickly from the room, leaving Miss Bingley to tap her fingers impatiently upon the table, Mrs Hurst to frown at her husband and that gentleman to call loudly for more kidneys. Shortly afterwards, we all rose from the table. Mr Bingley walked briskly down to the trout stream, while Miss Darcy and I went upstairs to put on our bonnets and walking shoes and take a turn as instructed by my employer.

†

We expected Miss Bennet and her aunt in the afternoon, but to my surprize, as we were returning from our walk, Mr Darcy came riding up to the stables. Dismounting, he beckoned us over.

'Georgiana, I fear you will not have the pleasure of Miss Bennet and Mrs Gardiner's company this afternoon. They have been called back to Hertfordshire on an urgent family matter. Miss Bennet wished to convey her sincere apologies to you.'

We stood without speaking for a moment, then Miss Darcy asked after Miss Bennet's health and that of her family.

'They are all quite well. Miss Bennet particularly asked to be remembered to you.'

He paused a moment, then gently put his hand on his sister's shoulder.

'I know that you are disappointed, Georgiana. We must hope to see them again before too long has elapsed.'

He turned and strode off towards the house.

I did not know what to think and I could see that my young charge was despondent. I too was sorry not to have the ladies' company. They were infinitely more well-bred than Mrs Hurst and Miss Bingley and my heart sank at the prospect of many more hours spent listening to Mr Hurst snoring while the sisters gossiped.

As we turned to walk back to the house, to my surprize, I saw Mr Hurst emerging from the mews. I could not think what business he might have there. He was very flushed in the face and his clothing was disordered. I averted my eyes and quickened my pace back to the house.

†

After dinner that evening, after we had withdrawn, I noticed Miss Bingley look quickly over at her sister and give her a slight nod. Mrs Hurst put down her book and addressed Miss Darcy.

'My dear, I cannot pretend to be sorry that Miss Bennet and her aunt did not come this afternoon. While there is no reason that they should not have claimed an acquaintance with you, Caroline and I feel that to pay us another visit was quite unnecessary. Miss Bennet's manners are rather too easy for our liking. And her family's connections are rather low. An uncle in trade, you know. We both think it best that the acquaintance be drop't.'

I felt the blood rush to my face. I turned to look at Miss Darcy and to my surprize, saw that her face had also changed colour and that she was gripping the arms of her chair tightly.

'Pay us another visit? Who do you mean by, "us", Louisa?' she asked in a perfectly calm voice. "Pemberley is my brother's house. If he chooses to introduce me to Miss Bennet and encourage the acquaintance, I trust his superior judgement. I was excessively disappointed that the visit could not be paid this afternoon. I find Miss Bennet most amiable and unpretentious and would wish to know her better, hereafter.'

I could not say which one of us was the more taken aback by this speech. Mrs Hurst turned red and looked round at Miss Bingley, who had also changed colour. Both ladies were staring at Miss Darcy as though they had never seen her before. My young lady rose to her feet and continued to speak.

'I did not go to a fashionable seminary in town and I have not the wide acquaintance of which you boast. However, I look to my brother for all which is proper and decorous and he has kindly engaged Mrs Annesley to be my companion.'

Here, she looked at me. I smiled at her, which gave her courage to continue.

'Mrs Annesley's behaviour since first we met has been a pattern for me to follow. She is courteous, ladylike and well-bred. She may not have a great fortune, or dress in silks and satins, but she is a true lady for all that. Louisa, Caroline, I wish you good-night.'

Turning on her heel, she walked out of the saloon. I followed her, my heart beating so rapidly that I thought it would leap from my chest. It was not fitting for my station in life to embrace Miss Darcy and tell her that I was as proud of her as I have ever been of any creature, but I took her hand as we walked up the stairs and pressed it.

As we said good-night, she looked into my face and said, 'Thank you, Mrs Annesley, for your goodness, your kindness and for shewing me what a lady should be.' We embraced and she gently closed her door.

I entered my own bedroom with a full heart. I am not ashamed to say that I shed a few tears before saying my prayers and retiring for the night. As I lay in my bed, I thought of all those I have loved in my life. My dear mother and father, my beloved husband, my little Thomas, the children I taught, Mrs Woods, Mrs Reynolds and Miss Darcy. For it was love I saw shining from her eyes tonight, and I was reminded of one of my dear husband's favourite Scriptures. 'And now abideth faith, hope, love, these three; but the greatest of these is love.[31]'

It is not vouchsafed to any of us to look into the future. I prayed most earnestly to my Saviour before I took my nightly rest, entreating Him in His infinite wisdom to look kindly upon Miss Darcy and Miss Bennet, who, I suspect, may soon be sisters. I also asked for renewed patience as my proximity to the Hursts and Miss Bingley looks likely to be of some duration. They shew no signs of ever quitting Pemberley. I can only hope and pray that the continued heavy rain will send them to the saloon to doze and play cards, while Miss Darcy and myself take a turn on the covered walk on the south side of the house.

I shall rise on the morrow with my heart full of hope, and continue to do my duty while praying that love comes to Pemberley, and in particular to my dear young lady.

---

[31] 1 Corinthians 13:13, from the Authorized (King James) Version of the Bible; however, I have used the word 'love' instead of 'charity'.

A GREAT DEAL OF INGENUITY

The Harrington Sisters

*Meryton society is lively, what with the five Bennet sisters, Charlotte and Maria at Lucas Lodge, Mrs Long's nieces and the two Harringtons, only mentioned once in the novel. In Chapter 39, Lydia tells us their names - Harriet and Pen. The context is worth examining. The two oldest Bennet girls and Maria Lucas have returned to Hertfordshire from Kent and London, respectively. As the coach approaches the inn, they see Kitty and Lydia looking out of an upstairs window, having come to welcome them. Squeezed uncomfortably together in the carriage on the way home, Lydia talks at top speed, cramming in as many pieces of news, gossip and reported speech ('My aunt Philips wants you so to get husbands, you can't think') as there are extraneous bandboxes and bags in the overcrowded carriage. In the middle of her stream of consciousness, the Harrington sisters, Pen and Harriet, are introduced as part of the gaggle of teenage girls who socialise and flirt with the officers. '... and Mrs Forster promised to have a little dance in the evening; (by the bye, Mrs Forster and me are **such** friends!) and so she asked the two Harringtons to come, but Harriet was ill, and so Pen was forced to come by herself; and then, what do you* *think we did? We dressed up Chamberlayne in woman's clothes, on purpose to pass for a lady. – only think what fun! Not a soul knew of it but Col. and Mrs Forster, and Kitty and me, except my aunt, for we were forced to borrow one of her gowns...'* The Harrington girls form part of the Bennets' social circle and are obviously more like Kitty and Lydia than Jane and Elizabeth, but are never again mentioned by name. I had lots of fun finding Harriet's voice and inventing an annoying older brother and a stern, but loving mama.

I WRITE THIS in a tearing hurry as Pen has a violent headache. We await a draught from the apothecary and in the meantime, I am walking to Meryton to meet Lydia and Kitty Bennet and see what news there is.

Since the regiment was quartered in Meryton, we have been going there every day, whatever Mama says. The exercise is healthful and although the roads are dirty in all this weather, there is always some new information to be had.

†

I am returned home to find Pen so much recovered that she is sitting up wrapped in her shawl looking out of the window for my return. 'You have been an age, Harriet!" remarked she, peevishly. "Mama had quite given you up. She scolded me for letting you go out again with the Bennet girls. She says we do not want to get a name for ourselves by running after the soldiers.'

I said nothing. I am sure I do not know what else there is to do in Meryton. I believe that Mama would be tolerably happy if Captain Carter or even Denny were to make an offer for one of us. I am sure William would be. Since we came out, he has been making sarcastic remarks about finding suitable husbands for us. I am wild to find a young man with two or three thousand a year who will take me away from Meryton, my hateful brother and all the spiteful old women. Mama says I had better learn to hold my tongue and to practise my music before I think of getting a husband. A husband in a red coat would be the best kind of all. He would not care about my performance on the instrument.

†

To the Philips'[32] for a little dance, supper and cards. Pen still has a slight cough but begged Mama to let her go as she hates being shut up in the house. Pen, Lydia, Kitty and I stood up with Sanders, Denny, Captain Carter[33] and the oldest Lucas boy who is agreeable enough although not at all handsome. Pratt[34] was indisposed. Mrs Long and her neices were not there which was a pity as they are very good sorts of girls. Even so, four couple is not so bad, even with poor Mary Bennet playing so ill. She was wearing a gown

---

[32] Mrs Philips, the Bennet girls' aunt, is Miss Maria from the first story, Mrs Bennet's sister.

[33] These are all young men serving in the regiment stationed in Meryton.

[34] One of the younger soldiers.

which I would not use for rags[35]! I wonder that her mother allows her out of the house looking such a fright.

Lydia came running up to us as we walked in, calling out noisily, 'Girls, you will never guess! You never will, so I shall tell you. Netherfield is let at last. And to a young gentleman with a great fortune. Mama says he has five thousand a year, at least!'

Miss Elizabeth Bennet looked over from the teacups to frown and shake her head at her sister. Lydia's voice is vastly noisy. Not one of us can be heard when she speaks, which she does incessantly. Pen, Lydia, Kitty, Maria Lucas and the rest of the girls clustered around me as we spoke of our hopes for a ball at Netherfield before too long.

What a thing for one of us girls! Mr Bingley is sure to be looking for a wife now he is come into Hertfordshire and all of us are out, even poor Maria Lucas who only came out[36] last year and is so shy that she blushes if you let out a sneeze! Maria's oldest sister Charlotte is likely to die an old maid, Lydia says. She is Lizzy Bennet's particular friend. She is excessively serious and very plain. She must be at least seven and twenty and may never marry. Poor Maria has little chance of securing a good match with *her* as an older sister.

---

[35] Harriet is being particularly scathing and rather bitchy here. Rags were used for sanitary protection in the eighteenth century, so poor Mary must be dressed in an especially unflattering gown.

[36] Young ladies entered society officially (thus leaving childhood behind) around the ages of fifteen to eighteen. Once they were "out" they could attend social functions and begin to attract the attention of potential suitors under the watchful eye of their mother or chaperone. Lady Catherine de Bourgh expresses surprise in Chapter 29 that all five of the Bennet girls are "out", not because of their ages (fifteen to twenty two) but because none of them has yet married.

Pen says that Lydia will be the first of us to marry, even though she is the youngest, and so she shall, I warrant. Mama says that Lydia Bennet is an impertinent young Miss. William says he would not be surprised if she should come upon the town[37], one fine day, at which Mama frowns most severely and hisses: 'William! Remember your sisters!'

We drank tea, ate muffin[38] and had a nice noisy game of lottery tickets[39]. Mr and Mrs Philips are vastly handsome with their hospitality and have a fine instrument so that we are always able to dance, even though we only have Miss Mary to play her endless concertos for us. Lord, how I should hate to be as plain as she is! How she will ever catch a husband I do not know. Still, with Lydia as a sister, she is sure to be thrown in the way of some young gentleman who will have her. A curate perhaps. How I should laugh if Mary was to become a clergyman's wife. I told Pen my idea in the carriage on the way home and she said that he could court her by reading her his sermons! What a thought.

†

Now here is a piece of news! Pen and I met Lydia, Kitty, Mrs Long's neices and Maria Lucas in Meryton this morning. Mrs Philips had been told by Mrs Bennet who told Lady Lucas who told Mrs Long who told her neices that Mr Bingley and a party of his friends are to attend the

---

[37] An eighteenth century term for becoming a prostitute.
[38] Not the sweet American style delicacy we know today. These were yeasty white rolls.
[39] A simple card game of chance often played at social gatherings.

dance at the Assembly Rooms next week! Our hopes of dancing were dashed when Lydia said that he was bringing twelve ladies and seven gentlemen to the ball. Seven gentlemen are not near enough, not even with all the officers present.

We all walked into the haberdashers to see if there were any new ribbons and trimmings come since we were last in there yesterday. There were not, but Lydia insisted on buying a very ugly bonnet which she said would do for Mary if she could not make it up afresh. Pen and I walked home, talking of what we shall wear to the dance. Mama has been promising us both a new dress for Christmas and it may be that she can be persuaded to advance us the money so that we can have new ones made up. Pen does not think that there is enough time, but she always looks upon the gloomy side of life. William says it does not signify what we wear, since no-one with any sense would want to dance with two such silly, gigglesome misses as we are. I wish William would marry so that we do not have to see his disagreeable face over the breakfast table every morning. His wife deserves him, whoever she may be!

†

I write this by the light of the candle as Pen snores next to me. What an evening has been had at the Assemblies! Lydia, Kitty and I danced every dance but one, Pen every one except the two fifth and two sixth[40], Mary none at all and Mrs Long's neices enough to satisfy *them*! My card was near full but I sat out the Boulanger with Pratt who brought me coffee.

There were not nearly enough gentlemen to go around, even with all the officers present. I believe that I looked very well in my gown, although Lydia Bennet in her worked muslin overshadowed me cruelly. I had hoped that she might tear it with all her caperings, but she did not. Pen says that is no way to speak of a particular friend, but I do not care. It is impossible to get five minutes' peace when she is in the room.

Lydia's eldest sister, Jane, was singled out by Mr Bingley, who is excessively handsome and charming! I would take him with three thousand a year and ask no questions. He danced with every young lady at the ball, even Charlotte Lucas, and was most polite and amiable. Mary Bennet of course did not chuse to dance, and spent the evening lurking by the fireplace and eating herself sick at the supper table. She looked a fright in her gown which I recognise from two winters since. I would not have been induced to wear it for any thing.

Mr Bingley brought his two sisters, a stout, indolent-looking gentleman who is married to the eldest, and a friend of his who is immensely handsome. Mama had intelligence from Mrs Philips that he is even richer than Mr

---

[40] At this time, dances were danced in sets. Couples would dance and converse, then dance again if asked. The Harrington girls would wish to dance every dance as it gave them the chance to talk to young men and meant they were not wallflowers, unlike poor Mary Bennet. The wording here refers to a particular set of dances at the ball.

Bingley, with a fine estate in Derbyshire and ten thousand a year! If I cannot have Mr Bingley, I would not be sorry to set my cap at his friend. But it was all for naught. Mr Darcy, as he is called, was above his company and refused to dance with anyone except Mr Bingley's simpering sisters. They were dressed in rich silks and I daresay their headdresses alone cost as much as Mama allows us to spend on dress all the year. I was disgusted with his behaviour, as were we all, saving Jane Bennet, who thinks ill of no-one.

Mrs Long's neices told me that he ignored their aunt completely until she forced him to speak, and even then, he looked very angry at being addressed. Mrs Long is a very sociable lady and entertains most handsomely at her house. She has a fine instrument and is always very happy for us to roll up the carpet and dance.

†

The next day, as we walked into Meryton, we saw Charlotte and Maria Lucas coming out of Clarke's Library. Maria looked like a frightened mouse, as usual (I would not wear such pale ribbons near the face if I had her colouring, but Mama says that Lady Lucas does not have the first idea of how to dress her daughters).

Charlotte looked tolerably well. She invited us all to supper at Lucas Lodge Tuesday se'nnight[41]. Mama had agreed to advance Pen and I the money for new dresses, so we all walked into the haberdasher to chuse our ribbons. I

---

[41] An archaic word for "week." Harriet means that they have been invited to dinner in a week's time.

selected a drab green, which I flatter myself goes well with my eyes. Pen insisted on turkey red, which merely brings out her high colour. I told her nay, but she would do it. William says that even in her first bloom, Pen is no beauty, but this is not kind. I am the pretty one, but Pen does well enough when she puts her mind to it.

†

Our lives are become a social whirl! Mr Bingley has left invitations on the entire neighbourhood for a ball at Netherfield on 26th November. Mama has agreed that we shall both have new cloaks, gowns, dancing shoes and hair ornaments for the occasion. Papa sighed and said we would be the ruin of him, but I believe he was joking. To be sure, nobody laughed, but Papa's jokes are not intended to be amusing. Lydia is wild for dancing and has ordered material for a new gown and capuchin[42] from the haberdasher. I would not dare, without asking Mama, but Mrs Bennet favours Lydia above all her sisters and denies her nothing. I am sure Pen would give a great deal to have Lydia's complexion. I would not be sorry to have her doating mama.

On our walk to the haberdasher, we met Captain Carter, Pratt and Chamberlayne. They are to come to the Netherfield ball. Captain Carter whispered to Pen that it is rumoured that Colonel Forster is actually going to be

---

[42] A cloak made from silk with a hood, worn over a gown. As the youngest sister, Lydia is spending money recklessly as the elder and more marriageable sisters should be given precedence on clothing for social occasions.

married! Who would accept such an old gentleman? He is older even than Papa!

I noticed Pratt looking sideways at me when he thought me engaged in conversation with Captain Carter. It is not seemly for a young lady to notice such things, but he has barely any whiskers and his skin is smooth. His eyes have a very grave expression in them which belie the curve of his mouth when he smiles. Stammering slightly, he asked if I might do him the honour of dancing with him again at the Netherfield ball. There is something for Miss Lydia to shriek about! I smiled and lowered my eyelashes as I gave my consent. He is the youngest and least consequential of all the officers, to be sure, but a dance is a dance and I find myself thinking of him as I fall asleep at night. It is only the very slightest acquaintance, and he cannot have a great fortune if he is in the militia, but he does look very fine in his red coat.

Our eyes then fixed upon a wonderfully handsome young man walking down the street with Denny. We were introduced and I forgot all about Pratt. The gentleman is a Mr Wickham, a friend of Denny's who has accepted a commission in the regiment. His manners were charming and gentlemanly. He bowed and said he would very much look forward to dancing with us at the ball. I am sure that he will look excessively handsome in his regimentals.

At that very moment, Lydia's voice was heard calling to us and there she was with her sisters and their odious cousin, a Mr Collins who is staying at Longbourn. Our attention was necessarily called away from our charming new acquaintance to be introduced to *him*!

Mr Collins is a clergyman with unremarkable features and a forehead bedewed with moisture. He is very fond of the sound of his own voice (much like his cousin, Lydia) and I do not know who has the job of dressing his hair. I feel excessively sorry for them, whoever they might be. I cannot imagine dancing with Mr Collins. As Pen said on the way home, he would do very well for Mary. I know that he will inherit Longbourn when Mr Bennet dies, which seems a very unfair thing to us. Perhaps he will make an offer of marriage to Mary. She sighed every time he spoke and was gazing at him from under her bedraggled bonnet. I have never seen her give a young gentleman a second glance before. Mr Collins has a very large nose and his voice is harsh and droning.

He cannot compare to our new acquaintance, Mr Wickham. Perhaps he will ask Pen and me to dance at the Netherfield ball. We cannot wait to see him in his red coat which is so becoming to a man.

†

It has rained hard for several days. The roads are so wet and dirty underfoot that we can find no employment but what the long days at home afford. I have sewed my seam, trimmed a bonnet, practised my music and listened to Papa reading improving works to us until I can scarce bear it. Pen and I are prevented by the weather from buying the shoe-roses[43] for the ball. We await them daily. How Lydia and Kitty go on at Longbourn we can only imagine!

---

[43] Decorations for dancing shoes.

✝

Pen and I are agreed that Mr Bingley is now the rightful property of Miss Bennet. He had eyes for no-one else at the ball last evening, which was very splendid. I have never been inside Netherfield in all of my life and it is the most magnificent and richly furnished place I could have imagined. Lady Lucas told Mrs Long who told Mrs Bennet who told Kitty who told us that the musicians had been brought from London! The supper was like nothing I have ever seen with dishes on silver platters. Mr Bingley must be vastly rich. It is lucky he is so fond of dancing and society and does not mind filling his house with slight acquaintances for a ball.

Mama chaperoned us and told me to accept Pratt's hand for only two dances. Papa spent most of his time in the card room with the other gentlemen and drank a great deal of port. My brother was called away on business for which Pen and I were devoutly grateful.

Almost as soon as we arrived, Lydia found us, dressed in her gown in the fashionable new stile with new hair ornaments. I wish that my mama spent her money so willingly on *us*!

'Pen! Harriet! You will never guess! Mr Wickham has been called away! I had promised him a dance, too! We shall have to make do with Chamberlayne and Pratt. I am dancing the two fourth and fifth with Captain Carter if you please! Look at my shoe-roses. Do not you like the colour? I was wild with excitement when they came!'

I noticed several people turning around. Lydia's voice is very noisy. Miss Bennet came walking over, took her by the arm and steered her to a sopha where she spoke earnestly to her in a low voice. Her mother and father never try to control her high spirits, Mama says. Mr Bennet was nowhere to be seen. Kitty says he would spend his whole life in his library if her mama would allow him.

We danced all night with the officers which was most pleasing. Pratt is a good dancer and very light on his feet. We spoke of the dance and the music and I can yet feel the touch of his hand on my waist.

The supper was elegant and the musicians accomplished. Mary Bennet would insist on playing and singing very ill. She wore an old gown and no hair ornaments and fixed her eyes on Mr Collins as she sang. Lydia's new gown was much remarked upon.

†

The day after the ball, we were walking to Clarke's Library with Mama. The rain had stopped and while the road was very dirty underfoot, Mama said that she could no sooner keep the two of us indoors than she could tame a wild horse. We were both glad of it. I longed for fresh air and some news. While Mama was speaking to Mrs Clarke in the library, Lydia and Kitty burst in.

'Only think of it, girls! Our cousin Mr Collins has made an offer of marriage to Lizzy and she has refused him![44]'

Mama turned around and frowned at Lydia. Pen and I would not dare to speak so loud in a shop, but Lydia never notices anything which does not interest her.

'Is not it a good piece of fun? Mama was in hysterics all morning and will not speak to Lizzy or even look at her. She keeps to her dressing room all the day long in a violent irritation of spirits and has been scolding Lizzy for being a disobedient undutiful daughter. Papa told Lizzy he would never see her again if she married Mr Collins. Who would? The nasty, greasy creature. Perhaps Mary can be prevailed upon to have him.'

---

[44] Modern readers of the novel are so invested in Elizabeth as a witty and strong-minded heroine that the implications of her refusal of Mr Collins' proposal are not perhaps as widely understood as they would have been at the time of writing. The Bennet girls and their mother are hanging by a thread, economically speaking. It would only take a fever, or an infection, or an undiagnosed medical condition to snatch Mr Bennet up into the great hereafter and in that case, his family would be homeless and virtually penniless. One would hope that the Gardiners and the Philips between them would see to their immediate comforts, but by refusing the man who will inherit the Longbourn estate, Elizabeth is being both brave and foolhardy. Had she said yes, Pride and Prejudice would be a very different novel, but Austen's original readers would have understood that, at a stroke, she had the power to secure the future of her entire family. She is playing a risky game, even with her manifold attractions (as her fumbling suitor points out), as she is gambling on a wealthier, more suitable man coming along and proposing to her. Saying yes to Mr Collins means her mother's fear of seeing another woman taking her place in Longbourn House would be alleviated at once. Married and settled in Kent, she would have the power to chaperone her sisters and oversee suitable matches for them, safe in the knowledge that Longbourn will pass into her hands (and those of her husband) when her father dies. Her decision to say no to Mr Collins would be discussed at every supper table in Meryton for quite some time, and the shock waves of Charlotte's acceptance of her best friend's cousin following so quickly on would keep even the most voracious news hunter satisfied for some weeks.

At this, Mama clicked her tongue and gave Lydia a look which would have terrified Pen and me.

'I take my leave of you. My compliments to your mother and father, Miss Lydia,' she said in a loud, clear voice, and taking us both firmly by the arm, she marched us up the street towards the milliner's. My heart leap't at the thought of buying new ribbons, but she was only interested in talking about linen with Miss Barlow. When I am a married woman, I shall prevail upon my husband to buy me as many ribbons and new bonnets as I chuse.

†

Several days later, Pen and I were engaged in trimming our old hats in an attempt to make them look new when Lydia and Kitty called on us with more news. Mr Collins has proposed to and been accepted by Charlotte Lucas, not two days since he was offering his hand to Elizabeth Bennet! We can scarce believe it. We talked and laughed and laughed and talked until Papa looked into the room and remarked that he had thought the geese had got into the house. This was another of Papa's jokes. We do not keep geese.

Mama says that Charlotte Lucas has made a far better match than was to be expected. She says that Mr Collins is a respectable young man with a rich patroness and that it must be a great relief for Sir William and Lady Lucas to have such a plain girl off their hands. It must thrust Maria more into society as well, which is no bad thing. Charlotte will be settled in Kent, which is a prodigious long way away from Hertfordshire. I should not mind, but I wonder if she will feel the separation from her family.

Lydia and Kitty were in excessively high spirits, talking and laughing of the uproar into which Longbourn has been thrown. I do not understand matters of law, but at dinner, Papa shook his head and said it was a bad business for the Bennets.

'I know not what will become of them if one of the girls does not marry well. What an unfortunate thing that entailment is, to be sure. And so Miss Lucas is to marry Mr Collins and leave us to live in Kent! Well, well. Sir William and Lady Lucas must feel all the luck of such a thing.'

I have never heard Papa utter so many sentences together at one time. I expect Mr Bingley will make an offer of marriage to Miss Jane Bennet before Christmas is upon us. She is very beautiful and virtuous and I am sure she is wildly in love with him. I would be. Pen and I staid up talking long after we had blown our candles out. Mama rapped upon the door and told us to go to sleep. I do not suppose that Lady Lucas will be long in calling upon us to share her good fortune.

†

We had scarce finished breakfast before Lady Lucas was on the doorstep. I do not believe that anyone has ever paid such an early call on Mama. Our new maid, who is very clumsy, drop't buttered eggs on Mama's skirt at breakfast this morning and I could see Lady Lucas noticing it as she walked into the parlour. She spoke for half an hour together of her delight at Charlotte's match, of what a respectable, sensible young man her fiancé is (I wish Charlotte joy of him, I am sure!) and of all the business of material and ribbons and bonnets and linens that is consuming Lucas Lodge. I cannot imagine that Charlotte, with her straight brown hair and unremarkable features will be the most beautiful of brides, but it is impossible to argue with Lady Lucas's rapture.

†

Lady Lucas had scarce made her farewells before Mrs Long was ringing the bell. She brought the news that Colonel Forster is to be married just after Christmas-tide and will bring his new wife to Meryton. January and February are always so dull. Pen and I are excessively pleased at the prospect of a new acquaintance. Mama says that she is a young lady from Ware, from a respectable family. I can only hope that she has lively and engaging manners. Our society will not much notice the want of Miss Lucas's presence, but another lady, especially one who is the Colonel's wife, must bring us fresh social opportunities.

†

Christmas has come and gone. Colonel Forster brought his wife to Meryton in January. She can be no older than Kitty Bennet or myself! She is not a beauty, but she is good-natured and friendly, with pleasant, unassuming manners. Mama says we could both benefit from following her lead and spending less time giggling and shrieking with Lydia Bennet. Colonel Forster is excessively fond of her. His eyes follow her about the room wherever she goes.

One evening at Lucas Lodge, Mrs Forster and I sat together on a sopha with our coffee. She spoke to me of her sister Eliza, whom she misses exceedingly, and of her mama and two younger sisters. She only met the Colonel last autumn when he came to her aid. It was a wildly romantic tale. I cannot imagine such an old man being violently in love, but so he is. Mrs Forster has a gentle manner about her and I would not be sorry to know her better.

She was telling me of her cousin, Fanny, but Lydia interrupted by seizing my hand and insisting that I come and dance with Wickham. We are all out of our senses about him. He is so handsome and charming and has such soft, beguiling manners. William teazed us about him at dinner last evening, saying that he is a wolf in sheep's clothing. Pen says she would not be sorry to be carried off by such a wolf as he!

†

Mrs Forster has promised to give a small dance next week. It is as well that she is come to Meryton as Mr Bingley has left Netherfield and is gone to London for the winter. Mrs Bennet is very angry with him and even more angry with Charlotte Lucas for accepting Mr Collins. I should not like to be Miss Lizzy Bennet. Her mother does scold excessively when she is out of spirits.

Charlotte Lucas married her clergyman at the end of January. The cold weather was not kind to her complexion. Maria had a red nose and Lady Lucas cried noisy tears of joy in the church. How I should detest to be married to such a man! I believe that Miss Lizzy has had a fortunate escape.

A GREAT DEAL OF INGENUITY

It is bad enough sharing a room with Pen, but the very thought of waking up each morning to Mr Collins' countenance on the pillow makes me feel quite ill. Mama says that Charlotte has done very well for herself and that handsome is as handsome does.

February and March passed away with more enjoyment than usually they do. Mrs Forster is proving to be a most delightful addition to our circle. She gives little suppers nearly every week. Even though she is the Colonel's lady, she does not give herself airs. Her lodgings are prettily fitted up, with plenty of room for dancing.

I called upon her one morning as I had promised to give her a sweet new pattern for a gown. I found her in the drawing room with a pile of correspondence on her table.

'I received a letter from my cousin Fanny this morning,' said she, shewing me a sheet of elegant, hot-pressed paper.

'I have not seen her since she and my aunt came to stay with us last year. She writes to tell me of the particulars of her marriage day and her wedding journey. Colonel Forster and I left for Meryton from the church door, and there was neither the time nor the need for such a journey for us.'

I had heard Mrs Forster speak of her cousin before, and I did not think that she was a favourite with her. I read the letter which boasted of fine clothes, jewellery, pin money[45] and carriages. The new Mrs Penshurst seemed to think of little but her new possessions and status in life.

---

[45] This reference implies that Fanny's new husband is well-off. Pin money was an amount of money written into a marriage settlement whereby the wife received a sum to spend as she wished on things she wanted but did not need. Therefore, Fanny is boasting of her wealth and disposable income, knowing that Harriet has married a man of good social status but less income.

'Fanny thinks poorly of the match I made,' said Mrs Forster, folding up her cousin's letter and sighing. 'Colonel Forster is older than myself, but he is a most devoted and affectionate husband, and I could not wish for a kinder. On the day before our wedding, he gave me a beautiful bonnet (the one you often see me wear at church, my dear) and these very ribbons. I had longed to have them, but our reduced circumstances made it impossible for us to buy such fripperies. The dear Colonel knew of my silly yearning for them and bought them for me as a surprize.'

She blushed slightly and cast her lashes down on her cheeks. I could see that she was reminiscing, and with pleasure. I had not thought that she returned her husband's feelings in such measure. She looked very pretty sitting there in her drawing room, with her cherry coloured ribbons and her embroidered muslin gown. For the first time, I thought that if I could find such a man to marry me, it would not matter if he were not so very handsome or endowed with a great fortune. Good looks fade, as Mama is wont to remind us, and to find a man agreeable and good-tempered enough with whom to pass one's life is perhaps more important than to seek a good-looking countenance.

†

Mr Wickham continues handsome and beguiling. Lydia was wild about him when first he came to Meryton, but he shewed no signs of partiality to anyone except Lizzy Bennet, and she is gone to Kent.

Lydia is forming a close friendship with Mrs Forster. I should have liked to have had her as my own particular friend, but she seems to be on terms of growing intimacy with Lydia. There are two years between them, but Mrs Forster is a very young woman, and unused to society, so I suppose that Lydia's high spirits and lively manners appeal to her. Pen and I think that Lydia is setting her cap at Denny, but Kitty says not. Mama says that Lydia will be lucky to find anyone to marry her with such poor prospects and so little sense. I have seen very little of Pratt this winter. He has a weak chest, or so says Chamberlayne. Perhaps it is just as well. As William often reminds us, neither of us can afford to marry without an eye to fortune and consequence.

†

Spring has arrived and we are able to walk most days without being up to our ancles in dirt. Mrs Bennet finds herself very dull with Miss Bennet in London and Miss Lizzy visiting the Collinses in Kent with Maria Lucas and Sir William. Kitty tells us that Mary is forced to come and sit with them all in the mornings instead of poring over her dull old sermons and practising her instrument. Mrs Forster and Lydia are now intimate friends.

I missed a good piece of fun through being confined to home with a violent cold. Pen, Lydia and Kitty dressed Chamberlayne up in one of Mrs Philips' gowns and caps! They passed him off as a woman at a little supper at the Forsters'. None of the officers suspected anything until Lydia and Mrs Forster started laughing and then the game was up! Pen came home to tell me all about it. Her shrieks of laughter made my head ache excessively.

†

My eyes are red with weeping! I shall never smile again. The regiment is leaving Meryton and is to go to Brighton for the summer! We have lost all our dancing partners and Mrs Forster and her supper parties. I am sure I do not know what we shall do. Papa says that the haberdasher and the milliner will surely go out of business since we none of us care what we wear now that the officers are gone. I shall see Pratt no more and our acquaintance cannot continue. I have not spoken to Pen of this. She would not understand and I cannot trust her not to tell Lydia, who would spread it all over Meryton. It is only the slightest of preferences, and I have no reason to believe that he returns my affection. I long to be married and away from William and his sarcastic speeches!

Pen and I are wretched. We will have only Lydia and Kitty, the Lucases, the Gouldings and Mrs Long and her neices to visit. I do not count Mary. I cannot believe that she plays so ill on her instrument with so many hours of practice. Lydia says her music makes her wild to escape to Brighton, but her papa will not hear of it. Her mama thinks that a little sea-bathing would set them all up forever, and I asked Papa if he would let Pen and me go with Mama for a week or two, but he only laughed and said that we did better at home.

A GREAT DEAL OF INGENUITY

I have taken up the tambour frame[46] once more. What else will there be to occupy my time with no officers and no Mrs Forster?

†

News from Longbourn! Lydia is to go to Brighton with Colonel and Mrs Forster! She is asked as Mrs Forster's particular friend. She not yet sixteen and yet I, at eighteen and Pen at seventeen not even considered. Kitty is in a violent passion and cries constantly. Miss Bennet and Miss Lizzy are come back to Longbourn and to what uproar have they returned! Mama says that Brighton will be the ruin of Lydia and she does not know of what her parents are thinking.

I ran to my room and cried when the news came. It is foolish of me, I know, but I had thought of Mrs Forster as a friend and although Lydia has taken her over, there had been quiet conversations between us which promised a greater intimacy. I say nothing to Pen. She would merely laugh and say I was a great fool to have thought that I could ever have anything that Lydia Bennet wanted. The worst of it is that she is right.

---

[46] A wooden frame across which a piece of material was stretched for the purpose of embroidering and beading. This was seen as a suitable occupation for young ladies and it may be that Harriet is thinking of a future trousseau as she plies her needle.

†

Maria Lucas is back from Kent and Mrs Long's neices have returned from their mama and papa's in Bedfordshire for the summer. Pen and I were expecting to find ourselves very dull, but with the families returning from London to Meryton for the summer, and the weather continuing so fine, we find ourselves less downcast than we had imagined. Kitty and Maria are less insipid this summer and we look forward to the ball at the Assembly Rooms on Thursday se'nnight.

A letter has come for me from Brighton. It is from Mrs Forster. I ran up to my room to read it. She wrote that her sister Eliza had intended to join her and Colonel Forster in Brighton for the summer, but that a private family matter had stop't her doing so.

'My dear Harriet,' ran the letter.

'I trust that I find you well and that all your family are in good health. We go on well here in Brighton, with balls every night and a large social circle. I find myself missing my friends in Meryton, however, and you in particular.

I wish to assure you that had Lydia not come upon me just as I received Eliza's letter, I would have asked *you* and not her to accompany us to Brighton. I flatter myself that we have enjoyed a close acquaintance and I would welcome its continuance. I told Lydia that my sister was no longer able to visit us in Brighton. She begged me to invite her in Eliza's place. Did I do wrong, my dear Harriet, by yielding?

Lydia is a pleasant companion, but I cannot help but miss your company. I often think of my time in Meryton and of our quiet half hours here and there.

I find myself often a little unwell and disordered at present, so am staying at home this evening while Colonel Forster accompanies Lydia to a ball at which the Prince himself will be present. How Fanny would stare if I were to tell her that her little cousin was mixing in such exalted company.

I trust that we will soon meet again.

Yr. affectionate friend, Harriet Forster.'

I am not ashamed to confess that I shed a few tears once I had read my letter. I seized pen and paper to reply at once.

†

It is late July now. High summer is upon us and it was Pen's eighteenth birthday last month. She shares it with Lydia, who was sixteen on the same day. I am now nineteen and I care not that I have no immediate prospect of marriage before me. Now that the officers are gone to Brighton, I have leisure time to sit and gaze out of the window into the garden. I often think of Mrs Forster sitting in her pretty drawing room in her muslin gown and her cherry-coloured ribbons, blushing at the thought of her husband's affection. Could it be that one day I will know such love? It seems unlikely, with so few eligible young men in Meryton, but if

Mrs Forster could find a husband on a muddy street while wearing a shabby bonnet, perhaps there is hope even for the Harrington girls.

†

Mama drew me to one side after breakfast this morning. I expected a scolding, but instead she said in a gentle voice, 'My dear, your papa and I have been most pleased with your behaviour since the militia left Meryton. I know that you were disappointed not to go to Brighton with Mrs Forster, but you have not allowed these very natural feelings to embitter you. I cannot help but be glad that Lydia Bennet is gone in your place. She is become a determined flirt and I would not have liked to see you continue to run after her and be involved in all her schemes and frivolity. You are a good girl.'

I knew not what to say. Mama rarely compliments us, and I felt tears rise to my eyes. She pressed my hand and smiled lovingly at me before walking back into the breakfast room.

I glanced out on to the street. Knots of people stood talking, their heads close together. Mrs Long was approaching our house, her cloak half unfastened and her gait uncharacteristically rapid. I wondered what could be so urgent that she was paying such an early call. The bell rang, insistent and clamorous.

I shall take my letter out into the garden and read again my friend's words. Whatever little local gossip or scandal Mrs Long has to tell; I am no longer interested.

The Cook's Tale

There is only the tiniest amount of information about this character in Pride and Prejudice. Her employer, Mr Bingley, mentions her in Chapter 11 and we learn that he is only waiting for her to make white soup enough before he sends cards of invitation to his ball around the neighbourhood. (White soup was a broth made with chicken or veal and its value came from its pale colour and expensive ingredients.) From this, we can deduce that she must be the cook at Bingley's new house. We hear no more of her until close to the end of the novel in Chapter 53 when Mrs Philips accosts her in Meryton to find out if the rumours that Mr Bingley has returned to Netherfield are true. I decided to make her a bitter, twisted character who has had a hard life and wreaks her revenge through blackmail and coercion. I had lots of fun researching the way medicinal herbs were used in the eighteenth century and, as you will see, I peeped into the elegant exterior of Hertfordshire society to see what lurked beneath.

Anne Nicholls is my name, not that it's any of your business. They call me, 'Mrs' despite my lack of a wedding ring. I have never been married nor wanted a husband. Men are nothing but trouble, good only for what a clever woman can get from them. And you, sir, have been foolish enough to put yourself in my way and for that, you must pay the price.

I know that you are very fond of my fine dinners here at Netherfield Park. Your breeches are in sore need of being taken out. No, sir. I am not yet finished with you. Please to take your seat again.

As a gentleman of fashion rather than fortune, you must be vastly pleased to be a guest in this house with its lavish hospitality. My master spends a deal of money on food and with such a soft-hearted mistress, I may buy what I wish and if some of the rich food intended for you remains in the pantry for me to enjoy, who is to say?

I learned my trade as cook when I worked for the Gouldings at Haye-Park. Do you know the Gouldings, sir? I squeezed all I could from them and when your brother-in-law, that young pup Bingley rented Netherfield, I made sure that Sir William mentioned me when he paid his first visit. I was engaged as cook the month before the young master moved in and I've been running the place ever since.

Sir William was glad enough to see the back of me, I dare say, but I knew enough about him to believe that he'd give me a good character and never say a word about what went on in the kitchens at Haye-Park. His silly wife spent all the day long gossiping and breeding. Ten brats in twelve years and her with no idea that there was a brace of little half-Gouldings in Kimpton, Codicote and Whitwell. I made

A GREAT DEAL OF INGENUITY

sure I kept in with all the tradesmen and farmers hereabouts. They know what goes on, and who doesn't welcome a handful of shiny coins they do not have to sweat and slave for? Money does not come as easy to servants as it does to fine folk like you, sir, with your rich clothes and indolent life.

Yes. I do dare. I will speak to you as I please, or would it suit you better for your wife and her family to know the true reason why no children have come to bless your marriage?

As you see, I have sharp eyes and ears and no piece of news evades me. From my earliest years, I have been seeking to advance myself and working for the smart folk, so profligate with their money, and their idle talk is a fine place to begin. Plenty of the well-bred gentry hereabouts sow their oats in strange fields and have dark secrets. I am never without a clean cap and a respectful curtsey; my head is full of knowledge and I know how to use it.

It is widely known that Sir William Goulding was not born the eldest son. He inherited through the early death of his brother from what the family put out was a fever. I knew better though. The apothecary, Mr Jones, told me he died of the horrors, brought on by excessive drinking and gluttony. And who was it spent late nights with him at the house filling up his glass and calling for more port? Why, Sir William himself.

Did you know that sir? I thought not.

Had it not been for his brother's early death, he would gone into the church or purchased a commission in a fashionable regiment, but now as the oldest son, he inherited the family pew, the house and all the lands and rents. He sits looking out over his fine park, drives to church with his fat, silly wife, his dolts of sons and his nitwits of daughters, keeps a good carriage and horses, and dines with all the neighbourhood.

As a man who has come into such good fortune, so very unexpectedly, why should he not pay the person who knows his secret and thereby keep his good name?

†

Mr Jones the apothecary has a half-witted, feather-pated ninny for a wife who cannot keep her mouth shut. Her foolish husband babbles the secrets of the good folk of Meryton to her and she in turn tells me. Who paid a visit to Mother Abigail in Kimpton Bottom, who is giving her husband a pair of horns[47], who is shewing signs of the French disease. George Jones has been known to me since I was a scrawny child living in the tumbledown cottages by the river in Kimpton, and he walking past and sneering at me, the addle pate[48]. I've made him regret every saucy word he ever said to me. He bows when I walk into his shop and he takes all the lavender water I can make and sells it at a good price. All his claims to respectability are in my hands, for I know his secrets.

I see you frown and wrinkle your nose. When did you last speak to a servant except to issue an order? The woman you see before you has come a long way from that puny little brat in the draughty cottage with rags stuffed in the

---

[47] A term for cuckolding one's husband.
[48] A dull-witted person.

windows and furtive knocks on the door at twilight. My natural father was a gentleman who took advantage of a poor little kitchen maid, scarce fourteen years of age. She kept her shame hidden for fear of losing her situation and the first her family knew of it was a fall of blood and a screaming baby on the floor. That was my entry into this wicked world, and no sooner had I come into it than my mother left it, abandoning me to the hard hearts of my grandparents who were forced to feed and keep me. I hate the soft-handed, idle, thoughtless ladies and gentlemen who keep the likes of me in our place. What do you know of want or hunger? Very little, judging by the ill-fit of your waistcoat, sir.

What is one little brat, more or less, in a cottage full? I was kept alive on second skimmings and scraps and reminded every day that I was yet another unwanted mouth to feed. Death was my play mate and disease waited around every corner. By the time I was ten years old, five children (my aunts and uncles) had died of the bloody flux,[49] fever, and fits. I was put to work up the big house when I was eleven. It was no better up there than at home, with blows, beatings and constant hard, grinding work to keep me in my place.

†

I had one friend, my mother's oldest sister, Lucy. She was eighteen years old when I was born. She worked in the kitchens at the Hoo and had a light hand with pastries,

---

[49] Dysentery.

bread and sweet delicacies which had brought her forward. She knew all the properties of herbs, plants and the wild things growing in the woods. To her knowledge of herbs and medicine we owed enough extra money to keep us from starvation. In the evening gloom, many a young girl would come knocking at the door to buy herbs to give her clear skin or heal an unsightly sore.

Affection and money were scarce in our cottage. My grandmother, as I must call her, was a miserable old fussock[50], my grandfather a stinking gollumpus[51]. He worked on the land for the gentry up at the Hoo, she cooked and cleaned and dropped brat after brat in between drinking and smoking her pipe. I was six years old when the last one was born, squalling and shivering in the foul air of the cottage. Lucy brewed up a mess of lemon balm to bring forth the afterbirth and I was set to cleaning the floor and sweeping it out of the cottage. The stink of the blood and the lye turned my stomach and I swore I would never bear children of my own.

†

In between dodging beatings and doing my work, I would wander with my aunt in the quiet, dark woods with only the birds for company. She knew all the places to gather tansy, mug wort and pennyroyal to sell to Mother Abigail down at Kimpton Bottom; wood bettony to heal wounds and broken bones; mint for drying up milk and easing the

---

[50] A fat woman.
[51] A large clumsy man.

pains of childbed; yarrow to stop the flow of blood and to ease toothache; sage for labouring women; tetter berries for stinking sores, scabs and canker[52], lamb's ears[53] and comfrey for binding and healing wounds and Queen Anne's Lace for those who wished to bear no more children.

Lucy grew herbs in the sunny patch at the back of our cottage. We picked lavender to strew on the floors, to flavour cakes and pastries and to make fragrant toilet water and tinctures[54] to sell in Meryton; lovage for brightening the eyes and cleansing the skin of young ladies hunting for husbands and thyme for all else. Our clump of feverfew was much in demand to clear the bowels at home and Lucy sold it to combat hysteria in fine ladies. Does your wife take it? If you do not continue to pay me, she may need to.

†

When I was nine, my grandmother died, leaving only Lucy, John, Mary and my stinking old grandfather in the cottage. Lucy still worked in the kitchens at the Hoo, John laboured in the fields with my grandfather and Mary was employed plaiting straw for hats and baskets which was all she was fit for, being a slow and dull creature. It was left to me to take over most of the cooking and cleaning and between the ages of nine and eleven, when I was sent up to the Hoo to

---

[52] Ulceration.

[53] The popular name for Stachys byzantine which was popular for bandaging wounds due to its natural astringent qualities.

[54] A type of herbal medicine very popular at this time, made from herbs steeped in liquid.

commence work, I learned the trade which has brought me a comfortable life ever since.

Fine ladies and gentlemen like yourselves cannot know the fear that grips poor folk. If the gentry who pay us decide to turn us out of doors, we have no power to oppose them. We must toil and labour all our lives to feed ourselves and never let the master or mistress know the burning hatred that blazes in our breasts.

Only to Lucy could I admit my true nature, for she too was full of anger and a desire to revenge herself on the half-witted, comfortable parasites who lived off the fat of the land. She schooled me in the art of pleasing, of wearing a smiling mask which fools all who see it.

'Remember, Anne,' she said one day as we were picking pennyroyal for Mother Abigail. 'Speak with a honeyed voice, keep your eyes downcast, agree with everyone, pretend to be their friend, present yourself as the perfect servant. You must listen at doors, flatter those who have knowledge, spy on others and find out all you can to make yourself the most powerful in the house. Never push them too far. Take what you can and be ready to move on when the time is right.'

I took in my aunt's words along with her knowledge of herbs. By the time I was employed as a kitchen maid at the big house, I was ready to begin my career of revenge on all those who had mocked us, laughed at us and used our poverty for their own ends.

A GREAT DEAL OF INGENUITY

†

For ten years I worked at the Hoo, and by the time I was one and twenty, I had risen to the position of assistant to the cook. I knew all there was to know about baking bread, sauces, roasting meat and fish, puddings and all the dainties the gentry love to stuff down their over-fed throats. I heeded Lucy's words and was become the ideal servant, polite, hard-working, demure and pious, whereas in fact I was none of those things. When the butler, Mr Shambrook, took prayers and said grace before dinner, I would glance at him through half-shut eyes and think, 'I know what you do when you think no-one sees you.'

Old Shambrook was a drinker, like all butlers, but more than that, he had an urge to feel the touch of young, forbidden flesh, to forget his own miserable self for a few seconds in the secret pleasures he took in his locked pantry. He was the first creature ever to pay me for my silence, and he was not the last. His companions paid me too, for the shame and guilt they felt was too great to risk a tattling maid telling all in the village.

I see you start, sir. Oh yes. I have seen sights which would make your fine womenfolk scream and swoon. I know everything which goes on in this house – and in the grounds too.

My time at the big house was my training. I left just after that filthy old brute Shambrook took an apoplexy[55] as he cleaned the silver. Fortunate for me that I was first to hear the crash as he went down, to open the unlocked door and

---

[55] A stroke

see his fixed and glassy eye, first to go through his pockets, take as much as I could carry then walk away with my eyes downcast, leaving him to be found by the scullery maid. I can hear the yells of her yet!

With Shambrook dead and buried, I had come to the end of my time at the Hoo. I heard that a cook was wanted up at Haye-Park and thither I went, a good character going ahead of me. The pay was greater and I had authority and power, possessions which make my heart beat faster and my cheeks flush. As other women long for an establishment and a man to provide for them, so I crave the power which only whisperings, secrets and shame can give.

†

Fifteen years I spent at Haye-Park, and a profitable time it was too. The master was in thrall to me, and it was not long before my knowledge of herbs brought me to the mistress' attention. She was often ailing, querulous and vain, with her silly useless hands covered in rings and her frilled cap covering her greying blonde hair. I made sure that Lucy's lavender water and tinctures made their way to the still room at Haye-Park, that I always had a poultice of lovage ready to bring the sparkle back to the mistress' faded eyes and plenty of the seeds of Queen Anne's Lace to thwart the master's desire to entirely populate the neighbourhood with Gouldings.

Lady Goulding had a sour-faced lady's maid who was ready to look on me as an enemy. I minded Lucy's words and spoke to her softly and beguilingly, flattering her skill with dressing hair and embroidery. Soon, the foolish gull[56] was eating out of my hand and I had license to give her mistress whatever physick for her ailments, real and imagined, I wished. 'I cannot do without Nicholls!' was her cry, and so my influence rose above stairs as inexorably as a creeping canker.

I was paid well for the work I did, and with the money Sir William gave me to keep my silence and the gifts of money and dress which his silly wife pressed on me, I was most comfortable. My idiot grandfather still lived on, mumbling and drooling by the fire while John took over his work at the Hoo. Mary, clumsier and duller than ever, plaited her straw and took to having fits.

After Mother Abigail took a fall by the bluebell woods one spring, Lucy took over much of her work, of which there was always enough to be done. Poor fools that young girls are, beguiled by the seductive whisperings of their sweethearts into losing their most precious possession. Many a maiden who spent her childhood by the bluebell wood is now robbed of her innocence, and will never smell the blooms again without a shudder. Lord, how it makes me rock with silent laughter when I think of it!

†

My reeking old disgrace of a grandfather died at last, pitching over by the fireplace and breaking his head. John took over as head of the family, not that Lucy or I need a man to tell us what to do. Thanks to Lady Goulding and her

---
[56] Someone who is easily tricked

many ills, Lucy needed hardly to peddle her remedies and toilet water in Meryton, making a good living supplying Haye-Park and many of the stately houses thereabouts.

I had achieved all that I could at the great house. Lady Goulding wept and wailed when I told her I was leaving to work for young Mr Bingley at Netherfield. 'What am I to do without you, Nicholls?' she sobbed, clutching at my arm while tears disfigured her lined face. I assured her that my aunt would be happy to work for her and so one Nicholls was replaced with another. I smiled to think that all my careful work with the Gouldings would not go to waste.

†

As I suspected, my new master was an easy mark. Young, rich, careless and with notions of entertaining the entire neighbourhood, I could see that he would be easy to manage. Netherfield was more agreeable than Haye-Park, with better kitchens and servants' quarters and closer to Meryton. Mr Bingley was considerably richer than Sir William, and with no wife or family to spend his money, he was happy to spread it around the neighbourhood in parties, balls and lavish entertainment. You, sir, have often been at this house and your carelessness has put you in my power.

A number of Mr Bingley's staff came from his London house, but my new master was most happy to leave the work of finding local servants to me. I chose carefully, ensuring that I hired those who were already in my service and those who could be manipulated into becoming so. Young Sarah Giddins was the under housemaid at Haye-

Park, and a fine little spy. She was vastly pleased to leave the Gouldings and come to work at Netherfield.

Mr Bingley was soon galloping off around the neighbourhood on his fine horse to pay his introductory visits. Sarah was the first to tell me that he was especially taken with the eldest Miss Bennet. They make a fine pair, he so rich and open-handed, her so simperingly pretty and yielding. Now that she is the mistress of this house, you are here with your wife and her sister for weeks at a time. I am always excessively pleased to hear that you are to visit, sir.

Mrs Bingley's fool of a mother is well known to me. She visited and dined with Lady Goulding often at Haye-Park and they are two of a kind. Querulous, complaining, silly and loaded with the riches denied poor folk. All they had to do was attract a suitable man, catch him in marriage and breed.

I knew that the eldest Miss Bennet would become the mistress of Netherfield. When my master was to come from London back to Hertfordshire last summer, her gossiping aunt saw me walking up the street towards the butchers.

'Good day, Mrs Nicholls,' said Mrs Philips, ready to quiz me, her beady eyes searching my face. 'I hear that your master is soon to return to Hertfordshire once he has quit London. When do you expect him?'

An express come from town told us that we had but two days to open up the house. I am well able to put on a smiling countenance when it might benefit me to do so.

'We hope to see Mr Bingley and his party no later than Wednesday, madam.'

'Bless me! Wednesday. Well I never. I shall walk to the butcher with you for we are in need of some game. We expect the Lucases tomorrow evening.'

I was in no doubt that my lady was lowering herself to speak to such as me only because she wished to extract the latest news. I smiled respectfully as I told her of the three couple of ducks I would order. I could see that she herself had wished to purchase them, but the notion of at least one of her neices marrying a wealthy man soon reconciled her to a plump haunch of venison instead.

†

Now that her two elder daughters are married and settled, while her youngest lives I know not how in Newcastle, Mrs Bennet and her family visit Netherfield frequently. I laugh to think of how you, sir, and your fine wife and sister-in-law must dine with them and play cards in the same richly decorated saloon. It is a fitting revenge indeed for all the wit Miss Bingley threw away on Mr Darcy, now married to Miss Elizabeth Bennet and living on his vast estate in Derbyshire. Even her affectionate heart and his easy temper must be strained by such a parade of visitors. While you are here, sir, I will continue to trouble you for the regular payments for my silence and I pray that Mr and Mrs Bingley will never quit Netherfield.

My store of coins is hid safe away in my comfortable room. I know secrets about the housekeeper which ensure I never have to do my own mending and that I take my nightly rest on a feather bed, like the fine folk in their gilded bedrooms. With such a pair of fools as your brother in law and his wife with their easy tempers and careless habits settled at Netherfield, I shall add yet more riches to my store.

I see you frown, sir. I merely speak the truth as I see it. I know too much of you to fear that you will pass on my words to those of whom I speak. I thank you for the bag of silver coins. You may be assured of my silence. I know what you do in the depths of the night while your fashionable wife snores in her bedroom and your brother-in-law sleeps the sleep of the just.

But I am too busily employed for any more idle chatter. I'll trouble you for the sovereign you promised me, thank you kindly. It wants but half an hour until dinner and I must put on my clean apron and cap and return to my work.

An Unremarkable Woman

Mrs Jenkinson is Miss Anne de Bourgh's companion, and may well have been her childhood governess. Certainly, we know that she supervised her young charge's education (clearly Miss de Bourgh was never sent away to school) and that she has remained with the family. To have Lady Catherine as your mistress would require nerves of steel and some fortitude, and there are some clues in the novel as to Mrs Jenkinson's character and past. We first hear of her in Chapter 19 during Mr Collins' excruciating proposal to Elizabeth Bennet. We are told she was rearranging Miss de Bourgh's footstool. Our first glimpse of her is at the end of Chapter 28 when she drives past the parsonage with Miss de Bourgh. Maria Lucas describes her as an 'old lady,' but to a teenage girl, anyone over thirty would probably look old. She next appears in Chapter 29, when Sir William Lucas, Mr Collins and Charlotte, Maria and Elizabeth visit Rosings Park together. '… and she [Miss de Bourgh] spoke very little, except in a low voice, to Mrs Jenkinson, in whose appearance there was nothing remarkable, and who was entirely engaged in listening to what she said, and placing a screen in the proper direction before her eyes.' At dinner (a very splendid affair as you would expect), she spends her time encouraging Miss de Bourgh to eat and trying to persuade her to try a new dish, while fretting about her health. We discover that four of Mrs Jenkinson's nieces have gained situations through Lady Catherine's recommendation, something which puts Mrs Jenkinson under yet more obligation to her employer. She plays cards with the ladies, as part of her role, and is obviously treated as a member of the household. So far, so invisible, but an important clue as to this lady's personality appears in Chapter 31. Lady Catherine is butting in on the conversation between her nephew Colonel Fitzwilliam and Elizabeth and begins lecturing them about music. She invites Elizabeth to come over to Rosings and practise on the piano in Mrs Jenkinson's room. Who plays on it? It cannot be solely for Mrs Jenkinson, so why is Anne de Bourgh not playing for her company? What is the exact nature of the relationship between Mrs Jenkinson and Anne? In answering these questions, I found myself writing this story of an unremarkable woman and her unexpected life.

IF TO BE REMARKABLE a woman must be beautiful, accomplished and graceful, then surely, I am the most unremarkable creature who ever lived. I was born plain, and disappointed my mama by stedfastly refusing to blossom into good looks.

My story is nothing out of the ordinary. I am the eldest of a family of three sisters and two brothers. My father was in trade and my mother had a modest fortune of her own. My one talent (apart from knowing when to stay silent) was playing the piano. My father was an accomplished musician and has passed on to me his love of music.

My two brothers were sent away to school while we girls remained at home with Mama. I alone of the family had inherited Papa's strongly marked features, aquiline nose and thick dark curly hair. On a gentleman, these features are distinguished, on a woman, repellent. A young lady looks to have a fine complexion, sparkling eyes, rosy cheeks and lips and a vivacious style of speaking. I have none of these admirable qualities. I am shy, reserved and cursed with a quick brain and biting wit.

My two younger sisters inherited Mama's good looks, but little else. In an attempt to fit them for the marriage market, they were set to learn the piano, at which they were no more proficient than I proved to be in polite conversation. I bitterly resented the time I lost at the instrument while they tinkled away, filling the air with their silly giggles. However, at the ages of eighteen and nineteen respectively, they departed our home to marry and breed, leaving me, the disappointing eldest daughter at home with my parents. My sisters will feature little in my story, so be so good as to think no more of them.

We lived in the small market town of Waltham Cross, as unremarkable as I. Mama insisted that we should visit the alms-houses with her once a week to distribute hot soup and shew Christian charity to those less fortunate than ourselves. With our fine clothes and smart bonnets, we would sweep in and look over the toothless old women and the pallid old men, Mama reminding us to stand up straight and not to touch anything. I could not have imagined then that I would one day be living in a fine house, surrounded by luxury and splendour, yet as much a prisoner as any of those unfortunates.

Miss Jenkinson I remained as my brothers and sisters married and moved away. My Christian name, Eleanor, is used only on the rare occasions my family take the trouble to write to me to tell me how my nephews and neices go on. My pet, my youngest brother Edward, died of yellow fever in the West Indies and since then, no-one has called me Ellie, which was his name for me. When Mama was expecting me, she was walking through the town and was struck by the Eleanor Cross commemorating a long-dead queen of England, this being the main feature of an otherwise dull and pedestrian place. When I was born, she gave me that name, hoping no doubt for a beautiful daughter who would marry well and increase our social standing. In that, as in everything else, I was a sad disappointment to her.

†

By the time I reached the age of five and twenty, it was evident that I was become an old maid. One winter's evening, walking past the parlour, I heard Mama and Papa talking.

'… Mr Oxborrow, perhaps, now that his wife has been dead six months. He is ill-favoured, to be sure, and has that great hobbledehoy of a son, but she may be able to catch his eye.'

'My dear, I do not think she would like him. He is a gentleman and comfortably off, but I do not think he would make a suitable husband.'

'Like him? She would grow fond enough of him once they were married and she would at least have an establishment of her own. Her only talent is playing the instrument and she becomes dowdier and more awkward by the day. Soon it will be too late even for a middle-aged widower and then what will she do? We neither of us are getting any younger. Charlotte and Anne will not want her. What will become of her?'

My father sighed. I heard him stand up and walk across the floor.

'We are not the only family in this town with unmarried daughters. I wish that you would not be so impatient with her, Fanny. I have been thinking for some time of writing to my sister in Kent and asking if she would be agreeable to a long visit. A change of scene would be beneficial to Eleanor and as you know, my sister is very fond of music.'

Standing outside on the stone floor, I became aware that I was shivering. It was partly the cold, but to hear my parents speak of me in such a way, as of an unwanted puppy or an ill-fitting gown, to be disposed of, hurt me deeply. I blinked away the childish tears which rose to my eyes and walked quickly to the morning room where sat my beloved instrument. Scorning the Scotch airs and Italian love songs which Mama favoured, I played my favourite Haydn sonata, now committed entirely to memory. Only music can soothe the anger which burns in my breast and is so wont to flame up into harsh words. I shall never marry! Let my father send me away to Kent for as long as he chuses! I shall not care one jot.

†

Bumping along in the hack chaise[57] over the muddy roads on the way to my aunt's home, I had no notion of the joy which would shortly be mine. I was welcomed most warmly by my aunt, uncle and their children. Their house, while not large, was comfortable and homely, and most importantly perhaps, no-one saw me as an encumbrance. Soon, I found myself teaching the children each morning and finding myself as a much-loved part of the household. My aunt visited everyone in the neighbourhood and welcomed her neighbours into her house for card parties, informal suppers and musical evenings. I was encouraged to play and sing as much as I liked. One lady in particular, a Miss Carter, soon became my intimate friend. She was several years older than myself, not at all handsome, but with a delightfully open countenance.

Our acquaintance rapidly deepened into real affection. We walked together, I played while she sang, we read to each other and soon found that we had a great deal in common. She too was the only unmarried daughter in her household, forced to give precedence to her younger sisters at all the balls and suppers in the county. One morning, arranging my hair before the glass, I realised that I was

---

[57] The Regency version of a taxi. Hack chaises were hired conveyances, ridden in by those who could not afford to keep their own carriage and horses.

taking more care about my appearance and dress than ever I had at home. I glanced out of the window to see Miss Carter walking down the path, her arms swinging freely and her cheeks glowing with the exercise. I stood looking down at her, my heart beating painfully in my chest and realised that she alone was the person with whom I wished to live out my days. To be her companion, to share a home with her, to support ourselves by teaching and by the needle, perhaps (for Miss Carter is very skilled in embroidery and the making of garments) would be most pleasing to me.

†

My time in Kent continued with no mention of my return home. My aunt came to me one morning after breakfast, a letter in her hand.

'My dear, I have heard from Mrs Shelvey at Cranbourne Court. She writes to ask if you might consider instructing her daughters. You know that she has four and their present music master does not suit. What a great thing for you, my love! The Shelveys are a very old family. They visit all over the county. I hear that they have even been received at Rosings!'

Rosings is an ugly, modern house several miles away, inhabited by one Lady Catherine de Bourgh. I know her by reputation as a most proud and haughty woman. I had no interest in such places nor such people, and neither did Miss Carter.

'I have seen her, of course. She believes herself to be a very great personage, with her carriage and her chimneypieces and her fine gowns. I wonder that Sir Lewis ever thought of her with that nose and chin!'

One afternoon, I was lying under a chestnut tree while Miss Carter read poetry to me. What joy, what delight! The birds sang overhead, the sun's dappled shade fell upon us and Miss Carter's soft hand gently turned the leaves of her book. I wished never to return home to Mama, although I felt the occasional pang thinking of Papa, who had always been kind to me. While I could earn my own money and be useful, I could not be wanted at home and the joy of having an intimate friend with whom to spend my precious time away from my little charges filled me with a happiness new to me.

Mama, it seemed, did not agree. Her letters spoke of illness in Waltham Cross, of the death of my youngest neice from consumption and of my sister Charlotte's fading health. My brothers-in-law got children upon my sisters on a yearly basis and I was now the aunt to many neices and nephews. Mama wrote that I was needed to run errands for her, to visit my sister Charlotte's household and to support her in her trouble. I entreated my aunt and uncle to let me stay where I could be useful and happy. They were beginning to relent when an express arrived one evening bringing the news that Mama herself had been carried off by the quinsy[58] and that Papa lay gravely ill. I wept, not so much from grief but from the fear of being taken away from Miss Carter and our happiness in Kent. Two days later, the

---

[58] Quinsy is a condition where infection spreads from a tonsil to the surrounding area. An abscess forms between the tonsil and the wall of the throat. As with any untreated infection in the eighteenth century, pre antibiotics, this relatively minor issue could prove fatal, as it does in this case.

news reached us that Papa too had succumbed and that I was now an orphan.

†

Wearing mourning for Mama and Papa and my little neice, the face which looked at me from the glass in my room was paler than ever, with dark circles under the eyes. I spent very little of my allowance on dress, and to be relieved of the necessity to choose a different coloured gown each morning was a comfort to me. My aunt and uncle were very kind to me, but I could only succumb to bursts of tears when in the company of my dear Miss Carter. It was agreed that I would go to live at Cranbourne Court and take on the role of governess to my young charges. There could be no question of me returning to Hertfordshire. Our household was to be broken up, much of the furniture sold, and there was no room for me at my sisters' houses. I had a little money of my own, but the prospect of working for my living heartened me. The Shelveys were an old county family, comfortably off, well thought of and kindly in disposition. I had my own room and parlour and license to practice on their instrument whenever I chose. My duties were not onerous and my little charges were well-mannered and charming. It was just over a mile of easy walking to the village where lived Miss Carter and she often came to pay visits to myself and the family and in turn I visited her when I could be spared from my duties.

I lived in this happy way for six months. We had settled between us that we wished to form an establishment together when I had saved enough money. We would live by teaching and our needles, supported by my little fortune and her meagre yearly income. Our needs were very few.

†

When I was a little girl, we would attend church each Sunday with Mama and Papa. The discourse was always most trying to my feelings, the clergyman's voice droning on and on and using words which I did not understand. Mama would frown at me whenever I swung my short legs or fidgeted and on the way home, she would speak severely to me about the need for a young lady to behave with perfect propriety in public.

'God has been so benevolent as to place you in a most fortunate situation, Eleanor. You may not have good looks, but you are a respectable young lady with some accomplishments. You must try to improve your character and be less sullen and dull. Conversation is important and once you are out, you will be expected to take your share of it.'

Privately, I had no particularly good opinion of God. He had seen fit to bless my younger sisters with beauty and lively characters, while giving me plain features and a resentful temper. I swung my legs no more but privately resolved to take no further notice of what was said in the sermon.

†

Christmas came and went and with it came the news that one of my nephews, aged but four, had also succumbed to consumption. Only Miss Carter's company and the anticipation of what was to come cheered me in the short, dark days.

It was a bleak, frosty February day. I was standing at the drawing room window, gazing out over the park to discern Miss Carter's figure. I had long been expecting her, but I attributed her unaccustomed lateness to the dirty roads and the heavy snow on the ground. The little clock on the mantel ticked loudly and the snow fell as the sky darkened, but still she did not come. I could not master a terrible fear which stole over me like a freezing grey cloud. I saw a figure on horseback galloping up the drive and recognised the Carters' manservant. He had come to give us the news that my dear friend had been struck by a runaway horse on her way to see me and was no more.

Thus ended all my hopes of happiness. I continued to wear mourning for several years, long after I could have left it off. My affection for her and hers for me had been a secret known only to we two and I could speak of it to no-one.

†

I continued as governess at Cranbourne Court until the youngest girl was out and my services were no longer required. Mrs Shelvey was too benevolent an employer to cast me out, and exercised herself in searching for a new situation which might suit me. I was now six and thirty, plainer than ever and with no charms which could attract even the most ill-favoured and desperate of widowers. One morning, as I sat with the second eldest girl, helping her to trim a bonnet for her trousseau, Mrs Shelvey came walking in with a letter in her hand.

'Such news, Miss Jenkinson. Lady Catherine de Bourgh herself is looking for a governess for her daughter. Only to think, my dear! The de Bourghs are one of the first families in the county. What an opportunity for you.'

It seemed that I should express joy, which I duly did. Privately, my heart sank at the prospect of living under such a roof, but it was most unlikely that I would secure the position to such a grand lady. Not three weeks later, however, I was packing up my trunk and preparing for the journey to Rosings to take up my new role as governess to Miss Anne de Bourgh.

†

I fought back weak, foolish tears as the carriage creaked up the hill towards the fine house which seemed to perch atop the rising ground looking down on all it surveyed. I was met most civilly by the housekeeper, Mrs Baker, an amiable and well-bred woman of respectable appearance. She shewed me to my room and informed me that I was expected in the winter parlour to meet Lady Catherine and my new charge in half an hour. I should not be late as Lady Catherine had a horror of unpunctuality. I smoothed my hair in the glass, pinched my cheeks to give them some colour and made my way down the stairs with some trepidation.

My new employer was enthroned in her chair by the fire. I approached her, curtsied and waited to be addressed.

"Mrs Jenkinson, you are welcome to Rosings Park. I trust your journey was comfortable."

I assured her that it had been. She waved her hand at a smaller chair by the fire which contained a small, pale, miserable-looking girl of about twelve.

"My daughter, Miss Anne de Bourgh."

I curtsied again and was rewarded with a jerky bob of the head from my charge. A terrified looking little maid brought us tea and sponge cake. My new employer presided, cutting the sponge cake into meagre fingers and giving herself the largest portion. I noticed that I was now Mrs Jenkinson and smiled to myself at the thought that with the very least inconvenience to myself, I had acquired the name of a married woman without having to engage in the disagreeable business of matrimony itself.

Lady Catherine quizzed me for quite an hour, asking me who my family were, my mother's maiden name, the value of my father's estate, to whom my sisters were married, what had been their dowries and in what business my brothers-in-law were engaged. I felt all the discourtesy of her impertinent questions, but as a mere companion, my place was to be grateful and keep my true feelings hid from this great and benevolent lady.

Once all the sponge cake had been eaten up, I was dismissed and given leave to unpack in my room. It was a neat, well fitted-up apartment with views down the hill towards the parsonage at Hunsford. Perhaps most importantly, it contained an instrument on which I could practise and on which Miss Anne de Bourgh would continue her lessons in music. It was at least four times more expensive than the pianoforte we had had back at home in Waltham Cross and when I struck the keys, it gave forth a rich, sonorous note. I could see that I would have at least one comfort in this strange, new house.

†

At dinner (a much grander affair than anything to which I had been used), Miss de Bourgh continued silent in spite of my attempts to draw her out of herself and most of the conversation came from her ladyship. We were joined by a Mr Heathfield, the clergyman at Hunsford and two other livings in Lady Catherine's gift. He was an elderly, dispirited gentleman with snow-white hair, shabby vestments and the look of an alarmed sheep. I judged him to be around sixty years old and when I found in the course of conversation that he had held his livings for the past twenty years, I began to understand his demeanour. Lady Catherine has the power to bestow money and livelihoods on many of her neighbours. If Mr Heathfield is anything to go by, they must all be excessively grateful creatures. I blushed to hear his effusions on the many dishes and Lady Catherine's munificence.

I do not know how I will do in Rosings Park with such an employer. I have taken a most determined dislike to her. Her strong, well-marked features contain no trace of former beauty. I know not how she captivated Sir Lewis de Bourgh. Her nose is of a similar cast to mine, its size and shape so often lamented by Mama in my younger years. Her eyes are hawk-like and miss nothing. Since I am now part of her household, I must submit to her quirks and fancies, one of which is that everyone around her table must listen to her in a respectful silence while she holds forth on a variety of subjects.

'It is a great pity that you never married, Mr Heathfield,' she boomed at the quavering man of God. 'The parsonage is the ideal size for a family. How do your poultry and cows go on?'

With the exception of an unexpected visit from the local fox ('Did not you mend your fences as I instructed you?') and an outbreak of the staggers[59] amongst the parsonage herd, all seemed to be well. I nodded encouragingly at my fellow sufferer and received a weak smile in return.

For a mercy, the food at Rosings is plentiful and well cooked. Lady Catherine boasted of the dishes and pressed me to try those which were unfamiliar to me. I took my lead from Mr Heathfield and praised everything, which seemed to please her ladyship. Miss de Bourgh said nothing except to whisper, 'Thank you' when I refilled her tea cup. She is full young to be in such company, poor child.

†

As companion and governess to Miss de Bourgh, I am given more status in the household than the under-servants, but it soon became plain to me that Lady Catherine rules her domain, and the surrounding villages, with more of fear than compassion. Her daughter is terrified of her, trembling whenever she is in her presence. Let no one say, however, that Eleanor Jenkinson is quailed

---

[59] A bovine condition caused by low levels of magnesium in the blood, usually seen around calving time.

by the mere appearance of money and breeding. I soon learned that my employer required absolute obedience and respect and had the very highest opinion of her own intellect and understanding. My own observation was that she was ill-informed and dominating in manner, never missing an opportunity to remind those around her of her rank, wealth and status.

'Mrs Jenkinson,' said she, as we sat in the saloon with its splendid gilding, family portraits and handsome chimneypiece. 'I cannot impress enough upon you the importance of my daughter's education. She is descended from a long line of noble birth and aristocratic advantage. Her sickly constitution was a great grief to her father, Sir Lewis de Bourgh, but I insist – *insist*, Mrs Jenkinson – that she be made to eat the delicacies which are specially prepared for her and that she should take the air at least once a day. As the heiress of Rosings Park, she must be proficient in music, deportment, drawing, dancing and all the elegant accomplishments expected from a gentlewoman of noble birth. I have drawn up a list of the subjects upon which you must instruct her. I wish her to practise constantly on the instrument in your apartment. There can be no excuse for poor playing or fingering. A young lady of my daughter's noble birth *must* be proficient in music. She has a childish aversion to it, but I expect you to take no notice and to insist that she practises most constantly.'

I had very soon realised that Lady Catherine did not expect an answer to her remarks. I merely curtsied and waited to be dismissed from her august presence.

†

As I sat beside my new charge, her hands sitting limply on the keys and her thin little body drooping listlessly forwards, I allowed myself a brief moment of doubt. Was I capable of being a governess to this high-born young lady? At Cranbourne Court, my charges had been merry and engaging in their manners, well-bred and accomplished. Teaching them to play and sing had been a delight. Here at Rosings it was an entirely different matter. I took a deep breath and sat upright.

'Which songs have you learned so far, my dear? Would you like to play to me so that I may hear the level of your proficiency?'

The child turned her head and gazed at me. Her complexion is waxy and sallow, her eyes deep-set and grey, her hair lank and her person thin. She sighed and played a scale, very ill.

'Thank you. Did your previous master teach you any Scotch airs, or ballads, or folk songs? Perhaps "The Maiden's Air?" The pupils I previously taught were very fond of …'

I broke off as I realised that my young charge was in some distress. Tears were overflowing in her grey eyes and running down her cheeks and her entire person was trembling with emotion. She was speaking in a muffled voice. I leaned closer to make out her words.

'I cannot – please do not make me, Mrs Jenkinson.'

The family of de Bourgh is perhaps one of the wealthiest in England and their consequence and nobility is known throughout the land. It was not the scion of a great dynasty that I took into my arms, however, but a little child whose emotions had got the better of her. She sobbed for some minutes, soaking the shoulder of my plain morning gown with her tears, before drawing away and wiping her eyes with a richly embroidered handkerchief drawn from her pocket.

'My dear, what ails you? Are you unwell? Should you like to take a turn on the terrace?'

She indicated with a nod that this was her wish. I ran upstairs to fetch her wraps and galoshes, for it was damp underfoot and Lady Catherine had impressed upon me the absolutely necessity of protecting her daughter's delicate health. We walked for some minutes in silence and I confess I was quite at a loss for words. I had been used to an easy flow of conversation with my charges at Cranborne Court. The silent, awkward, unformed girl with her pale face and downcast eyes walking by my side presented me with a sad challenge. I resolved to speak about the weather and see where it led me.

After several minutes of determined conversation, I began to speak about the girls at Cranborne Court. I spoke of their enjoyment of performing on their instrument, their family circle, the hopes for matrimony entertained by their mother and their love of pretty dresses. Miss de Bourgh glanced across at me and seemed to be gathering her courage to speak.

'Do you enjoy playing on the instrument, Mrs Jenkinson?' she whispered.

Here at last was a subject on which I could converse at length. I told my charge about my childhood, my position in the family and my love of music. I must have spoken for five minutes together and when I paused for breath, I saw that Miss de Bourgh's cheeks had some colour in them and that a slight smile was playing around her lips.

'Mama has never learned, but she is quite sure that if she had, she would be a true proficient. She often speaks of music to visitors and to me and she wishes me to play and sing in company.'

'And do you enjoy music, my dear?' I enquired.

Miss de Bourgh cast her eyelashes down on her cheeks.

'I do, I confess. But my teacher would become very angry when I played a wrong note and she would shout and pinch my arm. I was too afraid to tell Mama. I tremble at the notion of sitting in company, playing, and singing. My voice is weak and I forget the notes with Mama staring at me.'

Here she broke off and looked down again. Her voice was trembling.

'I am not well, Mrs Jenkinson. My head aches violently.'

I accompanied Miss de Bourgh to her room and promised her a draught to ease her headache. Walking down the grand staircase, I could hear Lady Catherine's loud voice in the saloon and the quieter bleatings of the unfortunate Mr Heathfield. I had no wish to be seen, so picking up the skirts of my gown, I crept past on my way to the kitchen to find Mrs Baker, who, I believe, is becoming a true friend.

†

My departure from the family circle at Cranborne Court had cost me many bitter tears and while I am treated with kindness here, it does not yet feel like my home. In my second month of employment at Rosings Park, the house was in uproar as Lady Catherine prepared to travel to Hampshire to visit her nephew, Colonel Fitzwilliam and his family. Miss de Bourgh fell ill with a fever the day before she and her mother proposed to travel and Mr Potts the apothecary (terrified of Lady Catherine as we all were) advised in a quavering voice that she should be kept at home.

'But this is excessively inconvenient! My sister Fitzwilliam particularly wishes to see Anne! I am most seriously displeased.'

The fine feathers on Lady Catherine's bonnet wagged indignantly as she stood in state in the saloon. The apothecary, bowing repeatedly and unable to meet her hawkish eye, stammered out his reasons for wishing Miss de Bourgh to keep to her bed. Greatly daring, I spoke.

'Miss de Bourgh has a violent cold, a cough and a fever, Lady Catherine. I feel that it would be most unwise to force her to travel such a distance, even with plenty of wraps.'

My employer wheeled around and fixed me with a beady eye.

'Unwise? Indeed, you speak in a most decided manner, Mrs Jenkinson, for someone so lately come to my house.'

I said no more.

'This is most inconvenient. I have not been in the habit of brooking disappointment and my sister Fitzwilliam will be excessively discomposed.'

She laid her hand upon the vast expanse of silken fabric concealing the area where her heart would have been, had she had one.

'This disappointment has brought on my pains and discomfort, which is most inconvenient. Mrs Jenkinson, be so good as to tell Mr Potts that I will require my usual embrocation and draughts before I travel into Hampshire.'

Turning on her heel, she ascended the grand staircase in an attempt to scold her daughter back into perfect health.

It was at least two days' journey to Hampshire. Lady Catherine intended to stay for a fortnight complete and so as the splendid de Bourgh carriage - pulled by four perfectly matched black horses and with the footmen and the coachmen in gold livery - rolled down the drive the next morning, I calculated that it would be near three weeks before I saw my employer again. Had I been on speaking terms with God, I would have thanked Him most sincerely for his munificence.

†

With Lady Catherine gone, Rosings Park assumed a vastly different aspect. The footmen whistled as they laid out the breakfast dishes, the housemaids exhibited a more confident demeanour and perhaps most importantly of all, Miss Anne de Bourgh effected a rapid and most pleasing recovery from her illness. By the afternoon of her mother's departure, she was well enough to dress and leave her room and at supper, she was more animated than ever I had seen her. We dined with Mrs Baker, and with no Lady Catherine fixing her eye upon me and demanding her share of the conversation, our intercourse was most delightful. I could almost have believed myself back at Cranbourne Court.

A GREAT DEAL OF INGENUITY

Dinner was a merry affair. I find myself liking Mrs Baker more and more. She is a most agreeable lady and has been employed at the house for over twenty years. As such, she has known Miss Anne de Bourgh since she was born. For the first time, I heard my young lady laugh and I saw that her spirits were less dejected than ever I had seen them. I noticed the absence of the glass of fresh milk from the dairy which Lady Catherine insists her daughter drinks at breakfast and dinner. As I was about to ring the bell for the maid to bring it, Mrs Baker put her hand upon my arm.

'Mrs Jenkinson, I think I may speak freely before you. When Lady Catherine is from home, Miss Anne does not drink her milk, nor eat custard or hasty pudding or cheese. And as you see, she is all the better for it.'

The next two weeks were delightful. My young charge rose early each morning, exhibited none of the distressing symptoms I had observed in her (difficulty in breathing after dinner, an unsightly rash on the back of her hands, occasional vomiting and a derangement of the inner organs) and made very pleasing progress on the pianoforte. She has a natural talent and rarely have I seen a young person learn so quickly. We walked around the grounds every day and even drove into Hunsford in the phaeton. Miss Anne's complexion improved, her eyes which had wanted sparkle and expression became clear and her conversation so animated that I scarce knew her.

Mrs Baker and I spent pleasant half hours together throughout the day and from her, I learned that our mistress is universally disliked and feared throughout the neighbourhood.

'A better and kinder man than Sir Lewis de Bourgh never breathed, Mrs Jenkinson,' said she, as we sat one afternoon on the terrace watching Miss Anne romping on the lawn with the dogs. 'He was able to keep Lady Catherine in check, but with his death, all restraint ended. Anne was but five years old when she lost him. Her father doated on her. The want of a loving parent has affected her very sadly, I fear.'

Lady Catherine has a reputation for being remarkably sensible and clever, but it has been my observation that she is neither. I ventured to share my opinion with my companion who agreed.

'Her Ladyship is not often from home and her absence is greatly to be desired. Anne is so much happier when she is gone. I am quite sure that her mother's manner towards her and her insistence that she drink plenty of milk is the cause of many of her ailments.'

We sat in the warm spring sunshine, the gentle breeze ruffling our caps, and watched poor Miss Anne playing happily, her days of freedom numbered. We talked of many pleasant things and I felt a swell of happiness at the certain knowledge that my dear Miss Carter was not to be my only intimate friend.

†

My life at Rosings Park continued, one month succeeding another and the years slowly going by. Lady Catherine gave me leave to visit my family the first Christmas I was at Rosings and it was a sad sight to see my formerly lively sister Charlotte with greying hair, a sad countenance and two children less at her dining table. My elder neices, now fine girls of eighteen and seventeen, are in search of husbands, and with their good looks and dowries will no doubt soon be successful in their quest. My sister Anne with her brood of boys and girls lives in less stile and my neices will be most fortunate to fix the affection of any man with more than two thousand pounds a year.

Upon overhearing a slight remark at dinner made by myself to poor Mr Heathfield, Lady Catherine called down the table to me in her harsh voice.

'What are you saying to Mr Heathfield? I cannot hear you. You speak very low, Mrs Jenkinson. Of what are you talking?'

'Of my sister Anne, Lady Catherine. She has five daughters and we were speaking of the iniquity of the lack of suitable gentlemen for them to marry.'

My employer frowned, her hawkish features and large nose illuminated by the mass of beeswax candles on the table.

'Five daughters! A ridiculous amount. She would have done better to have sons.'

'She did, madam. Three of them.'

I was rewarded by another scowl and she took to scolding her daughter in a lower voice for not eating up her syllabub. As we drank coffee in the saloon after dinner, I was beckoned over by a be-ringed hand.

'I understand that Lady Weysford is looking for a governess for her daughters. Pray, how old is your eldest neice?'

I replied that she was eighteen.

'I shall write to Lady Weysford directly and ask her if she will consider situating your neice. I am always glad to get a young person well placed out. I do not suppose your sister will object, indeed, she will be glad of it, for the reduction in board and pocket will be considerable I imagine.'

Anne's next letter to me contained her grateful thanks. My neice Amelia, although accomplished and good natured, has not inherited her mother's looks and as such is ideally suited to act as a governess to a large family of children. I am yet further indebted to Lady Catherine, who, as well as paying me a good salary and giving me a roof over my rapidly ageing head is now taking it upon herself to recommend my neices to the local gentry. I can scarce contain my gratitude.

†

Fifteen years have passed. Miss Anne is now a woman of seven and twenty, as yet unmarried and still forced to drink milk twice daily in spite of her ailing stomach. Mr Heathfield drop't down in the pulpit of an apoplexy while preaching last summer and his place was taken by Mr Collins, a heavy, stolid young man of little conversation or natural intellect. Our family circle at Rosings Park is greatly enriched by his toadying and fawning conversation.

Miss Anne and I go on very well together. When her mother is from home (which is not nearly often enough, in my opinion) she plays the pianoforte with as much fire and passion as ever I did. The thin, trembling, frightened little girl is now a woman with a mind of her own, which, sadly, she must keep concealed from her mother. When called upon to play, she will do so only in front of her immediate family. This enrages her mother who suffers from increasing chest pains brought on by rage and disappointment.

Lady Catherine continues loud and dominating, scolding the cottagers into plenty and interfering in her neighbours' affairs. In January we welcomed Mr Collins' new wife to Hunsford; the parsonage was fitted up and smart furnishings bestowed upon it by the new incumbent's noble patroness. Mr Collins' gratitude on the subject is apparently endless. Mrs Collins is a sensible and agreeable woman and I believe I detect considerable intelligence in her. I cannot understand why she married such a dolt as her husband, but when a young lady is plain and without a good dowry, her choice in marriage is necessarily limited.

Mrs Collins' friend, a Miss Elizabeth Bennet, came to visit her friend at Hunsford, along with Mrs Collins' father and sister in March. Mr Darcy and Colonel Fitzwilliam were staying with us at Rosings Park at the time and I marvelled at Lady Catherine's blindness to the contempt in which at least one of her nephews holds her. Anne and I spoke long into the night about the Colonel's obvious preference for Miss Bennet. I do not believe that he will make her an offer of marriage. He cannot take a wife where he chuses, although he clearly admires her very much. Mr Darcy, we both noticed, spent a great deal of time in conversation with the young lady and fixed his eyes upon her when she played and sang. Miss Anne has taken a violent fancy to Miss Bennet but is too shy to speak much to her when we are in company together or to play upon the instrument in front of her cousins. Her mother, on the other hand, seems to regard the young lady as rather impertinent. She plays and sings delightfully, in spite of a poor notion of fingering. I wish my own dear young lady had the courage to exhibit in company. What compliments would then flow in!

✝

It has long been Lady Catherine's desire that her daughter marry her silent and imposing cousin, Mr Darcy, but it is my belief that she will wait until her mother is no more and make her own choice. She has no particular liking for Mr Darcy and he none at all for her. Certainly, I will be there to support her in whatever decision she makes. Rarely have I met a stronger-minded woman, made all the more so by the need to conceal her true character from Lady Catherine.

Mrs Baker and I conspire to make her life more bearable. The cows often fail to produce milk (so says our excellent housekeeper) and Mr Potts has been persuaded to assure Lady Catherine that a diet rich in fruit will benefit her daughter's health. We take long walks around the park and ride out in her little phaeton whenever we can to escape from the useless finery and rich furnishings at Rosings.

'When I am allowed to be the true mistress of Rosings Park, Mrs Jenkinson, I shall tear down the velvet curtains and put an instrument in every room. There shall be fruit from the hothouses at every meal and I will dismiss Mr Collins at once, for his fawning servitude and harsh voice makes my head ache. I shall play upon the pianoforte every day and rise when I please.'

Would that my young lady had the strength to confront her mother, but I fear this will never happen. We shall have to wait until Lady Catherine is snatched up to heaven (or a region adjacent to it) before her daughter is allowed to take her rightful place as the owner of Rosings Park.

I am grown very fond of Mrs Collins and I would not wish to see her turned out of the parsonage, especially, if as I suspect, she is with child. My young lady is of a naturally kindly disposition, but I do understand that a lifetime lived with Lady Catherine would be enough to sour the sweetest of characters.

Of late, Mr Collins' noble patroness has been complaining more and more of severe pains in her chest. Were I a pious woman, I would pray that she is spared to us for many more years. However, when Lady Catherine is no more, her daughter will be mistress at Rosings, with the power to direct her own life and dispose of her fortune as she chuses. Her faithful companion will be by her side, the ill-favoured Miss Eleanor Jenkinson, now elevated to the rank of companion to one of the richest and well born young ladies in England. An unremarkable woman I may be, but fate has conspired to place me in a more remarkable situation than ever I could have dreamed of.

Mrs Long and Her Neices

We know extraordinarily little of Mrs Long and yet she has inspired the most detailed character introduction in this book, based on the tantalising clues about her scattered throughout Pride and Prejudice. Austen paints a lively picture of Meryton society with several principal figures in the town itself, the Lucases a mile or so away at Lucas Lodge and the Bennets within an easy walk of the town at Longbourn. The remainder of the four and twenty families with whom they dine, presumably, are scattered around the district. Mrs Long's nieces form part of the group of excitable teenage girls with Lydia Bennet at their head and although, or perhaps because, they are never named or given a word of dialogue, they have always fascinated me. Mrs Long herself is the third person to be mentioned by name, straight after the Bennets. We have only just read the famous opening remarks about a single man in possession of a good fortune when we are plunged straight into a conversation between Mr and Mrs Bennet. Mrs Long clearly knows every single delightful detail about Mr Bingley. She has made a beeline for Longbourn ('... Mrs Long has just been here, and she told me all about it') and poured each juicy nugget of news into

Mrs Bennet's eagerly waiting ear. A young man of large fortune from the north of England is coming to the neighbourhood, which makes him fair game for all the matchmaking mamas round and about the district. Mrs Long has done her research. She knows that he visited on Monday in a chaise and four (a sure sign of wealth – a person needed to have at least £1,000 a year to afford their own carriage and the four horses indicate that he has no money worries and likes to travel at speed. These days, he would be driving a Tesla). Further, she reveals, he loved Netherfield so much that he's agreed a moving in date with the local land agent (Mr Morris), will be in residence by Michaelmas (29th September) and is sending some of his servants down to open up the house at once. Mrs Bennet has an indefatigable ear for news, plus the benefit of her sister Philips, conveniently located in the heart of Meryton, yet Mrs Long is clearly the winner in the news stakes here. Is she acquainted with Mr Morris, the land agent? Does she know Mrs Nicholls, the cook at Netherfield? She is the character with the privilege of kicking off the narrative, but is given little else to do throughout the book. She is probably a widow, since in Chapter 53, just after Lydia and Wickham's marriage, Mrs Bennet says, 'We must have Mrs Long and the Gouldings soon [to dinner].' As such, with no husband to make the first courtesy visit to Bingley, presumably she does it herself, as in Chapter 2, Elizabeth reassures her mother that Mrs Long has promised to introduce them at the assemblies. This gives her a huge advantage over Mrs Bennet and we further learn that she has two unmarried nieces, very likely the reason for Mrs Bennet's spiteful outburst. 'She is a selfish, hypocritical woman, and I have no opinion of her.' It may well be that

Mrs Long has got her eye on Netherfield Park for one of her own nieces. In Chapter 54, she and the girls must be of the party who visit Longbourn just before Jane and Bingley become engaged. In the self-satisfied glow of very nearly having a daughter well married, Mrs Bennet refers to them as 'very pretty behaved girls, and not at all handsome: I like them prodigiously.' Now that they are no longer rivals in the Bingley marriage stakes, she is free to treat them with perfect civility once more, also complimenting Mrs Long as: '... as good a creature as ever lived.' Writing this story also gave me the opportunity to shine a light on the Lucas and Collins households. We are told relatively little about the Lucases in the novel (Austen focuses mainly on Charlotte, with Sir William and Maria making several appearances), but I sent Mrs Long, that doughty searcher out of gossip, off to Lucas Lodge when the lady of the house was absent. This gave me the ideal opportunity, dear reader, to worry out some intriguing snippets of news about life at Hunsford Parsonage. Mrs Long, naturally, would be delighted to hear about a potential suitor for Maria, as that would reduce the number of marriageable young ladies left in Meryton as rivals to her nieces. Having read and re-read the novel many times, I found Mrs Long taking shape, a robust, essentially kind-hearted woman with a hearty appetite for tea and all its accompaniments, a native of Meryton whose story I could not wait to tell.

A GREAT DEAL OF INGENUITY

As I was saying to Lady Lucas just the other day, never have I known such excitement. The last twelvemonth has brought scandal, elopement, gossip, news and several marriages to Meryton and although I am no longer a young woman, I own that I have taken great enjoyment in learning all the news.

'My dear Mrs Long,' said Lady Lucas to me as we drank tea and nibbled on seed cake in the parlour at Lucas Lodge. 'Never did I think that my own Charlotte would one day be married and settled so far from me and now here is Jane Bennet married very well and living at Netherfield Park and her sister the mistress of a great estate up in the north of the country. To be sure, we must look for suitable young men for my own Maria and your neices, Dorothea and Catherine.'

She paused and held up her handkerchief in front of her mouth for a moment. I am very fond of seed cake, but one needs to spend some time alone after consuming it as the seeds are most injurious to the teeth. I much prefer the tea bread and lemon tarts at Longbourn. Mrs Hill is a fine cook, although Lady Lucas' Mrs Mason is known for her mince pies and her masterful way with a haunch of venison. With such a numerous family and a respectable name to keep up in the neighbourhood, the Lucas girls have more to do in the kitchen than either of my nieces or any of the Bennets and it is as well that Mrs Mason is so good-natured.

Having removed the seed, Lady Lucas adjusted her cap and leaned forward to poke the fire. For a woman with such a numerous family and limited fortune, she is most prodigal indeed with her coals. I have not had the fire lit in my bedroom since April.

'Do not you think, my dear, that Dorothea may have caught the eye of young Mr Goulding? I noticed he danced three dances with her at the assemblies last week and I must say she was in very good looks. There will be a fine match if it comes off.'

I have every intention of catching Thomas Goulding for Dorothea. He is tolerably handsome, most amiable and if not the cleverest young man in the neighbourhood, he will at least have a good fortune. I have laid out a considerable sum in fine family suppers and card parties at my house and he is shewing a most promising affection for my neice who plays and sings like an angel. I saw no need to tell Lady Lucas, however, since she would walk immediately to Longbourn and pour my own particular news into the ear of Mrs Bennet, a gossip and busybody if ever I saw one. I adjusted my fichu and prevaricated.

'I do not know, my dear. He danced with your Maria several times and he also stood up with the Harrington girls and Mary and Kitty Bennet.'

This of course was only common courtesy. No well-bred young man would leave ladies in want of a partner at a dance, even if they were as plain and dull as poor Mary Bennet who spends far more time practising at her wretched instrument than she ever does in front of her glass. Now that no less than three of her sisters are married and settled, however, she and Miss Kitty must spend a good deal more of their day with their mother. Since Miss Lydia became Mrs Wickham in that disgraceful, hushed-up way in the summer and Miss Bennet and Miss Elizabeth Bennet were married at Christmas, their mother has been less in the fidgets than ever I have seen her. Longbourn House is the quietest ever I have known it since Miss Gardiner married Mr Bennet four and twenty springs ago.

Dorothea and Catherine went home to my sister and brother at Christmas and they are returned now that summer is almost upon us and visiting and parties are recommenced. Dorothea is two and twenty and Catherine twenty and they are very good, agreeable girls. Without Mrs Bennet pushing her daughters in front of my neices at every dance we attend, I think I shall do very well this year. I have all but promised my sister that I shall have at least one of them engaged before Michaelmas.

†

It is an easy walk from Lucas Lodge into Meryton. When a woman is in excellent health and has a stout pair of walking shoes, she need not fear a brisk tramp from one house to another. The birds were singing joyfully and the cow parsley frothing along the border of the lane as I strode along. When I was a young, unmarried girl, my mother would scold me for the grass stains and tears I inflicted upon my gowns. I did not enjoy the more ladylike pursuits of embroidery and singing like my sister (an acknowledged beauty) but loved nothing more than exploring the beautiful countryside around Meryton.

When Colonel Miller's regiment was quartered in the town, Mama forbade me from continuing my solitary rambles. I was forced to spend more time with the giggling misses who were husband hunting, including Miss

Gardiner and Miss Maria Gardiner. Once Mr Bennet of Longbourn House had been captivated and safely wed, there were fewer suitable young gentlemen left for us all to marry. Mr William Lucas had, of course, been captured several years before that to the annoyance of my mama who had her eye on him for my sister. Miss Maria made do with her father's clerk and lives still in the house where she was born. It was her abode to which I now hurried.

Mrs Philips is a very good kind of woman, not clever, certainly, but amiable enough. Her cook makes the most delicious rout cakes[60], sweet and soft, filled with currants and well flavoured with orange water. When my hostess saw me approaching, she threw up her parlour window and loudly hailed me.

'My dear Mrs Long! Do come in. I have such news.'

I noticed Mrs Nicholls, the cook at Netherfield House, turn her head at this. She was walking out from the butcher's, her basket filled with meat. I do not trust her. She has a watchful eye and a sharp tongue. I rang the bell and walked in, handing my pelisse[61] and walking boots to the maid and putting my stockinged feet into my slippers.

I was ushered into the parlour which commands such a fine view of Meryton and all its citizens. Mrs Philips misses not a single scrap of local news and dines with six and twenty families at least. She is nearly always sure to know of a flirtation, an engagement or a scandal just after I learn

---

[60] Small, soft cakes made with flour, butter, sugar, currants, eggs, rose water, wine and brandy. Often served with butter and/or jam.

[61] A long coat worn by women over their gowns throughout the eighteenth and well into the nineteenth century. It was sometimes fur-lined (Lady Catherine and her daughter would certainly have insisted on this refinement) and could have a hood.

of it, for I have the sharpest eyes and keenest ears in all of Meryton. I was eager to hear of her news and vastly pleased to see her little maid bring in tea and a plate of the aforementioned rout cakes.

'How do you all go on, my dear? I thought Dorothea in very good looks at the assemblies last week. Thomas Goulding shews a very promising affection for her, does he not? How happy you would be to have a neice well married and settled so close to you!'

She said all this while pouring the tea and offering me a rout cake. I took a bite. Delicious. Mrs Philips continued without taking a breath.

'How does Charlotte Collins do? Lady Lucas will be looking around for a good match for Maria now that Charlotte is disposed of. She must be near to being brought to bed[62] is not she?'

Mrs Philips and I have known each other since we were girls and with no gentlemen within earshot, we were able to speak freely of subjects which are quite unsuitable for young unmarried ladies. Mrs Collins expects her first child imminently. Lady Lucas is leaving for Kent on the morrow with Maria as her companion and expects to be in Hunsford by Wednesday. We will have so much news when she returns! A new baby and no doubt stories of drinking tea and dining at Rosings Park. Charlotte did well to secure such a good match – the Lucas girls are nearly all very plain and poor Maria is sadly in want of that wit and vivacity which attracts young men.

---

[62] Archaic term meaning to give birth.

Mrs Philips and I are both in agreement that Lady Lucas does not know how to dress her daughters. Miss Louisa Lucas is now sixteen years of age and just out and wears colours which make her pale face with its pointed chin and prominent eyes even paler. But she and Miss Lucas have an older sister well married and the opportunity to visit their sister's household in Kent whenever they chuse. Lady Lucas does well to take Maria with her to Hunsford. We may hear of an engagement before too long. Surely there is a respectable curate or even the younger son of a baronet who may notice Miss Lucas. To have two daughters married and settled in the same county would be a splendid thing indeed for Sir William and Lady Lucas. It may even be that their oldest son would prove to be a tolerably good match for Catherine, but I will see if any promising young gentlemen shew themselves this summer before I begin to make my play for a Lucas boy. They are a most respectable family, but few of their children have been blessed with good looks.

'So, my dear! You must know, indeed you must. I visited my sister Bennet this morning after breakfast. Such a fine day for walking. Mild weather and my light blue pelisse hardly required in such good sunshine. Kitty's cough is much improved with the draughts from Mr Jones and Mary was wearing one of her new gowns. You know our sister Gardiner has been visiting at Longbourn and she brought with her all the news of the new fashions and several bolts of cloth for my sister and the girls. Mary's morning gown is most becoming. I always told my sister, "My dear, do not dress Mary in such pale colours. She has such beautiful brown eyes and a deeper shade would bring them out." And I was right. She was wearing a charming dress, almost the colour of a fine old sherry and it did become her very well. She will never be a beauty like Jane, of course, but properly dressed and with her hair done, she is quite tolerable. I told my sister Bennet of Lady Lucas' imminent departure for Hunsford and she was almost amiable about Charlotte's confinement. Indeed, now that Jane and Elizabeth are so well married, the entire family could move to Netherfield or Pemberley should my brother Bennet die suddenly. Not that I believe he will. He looked in very good health when I saw him through the library window.'

I am accustomed to Mrs Philips' effusions. She is almost as fond of news as her sister and I took the opportunity to avail myself of another rout cake while she spoke.

'La, my dear! How I do run on. Let me tell you the news! You are the first to hear of it for my sister Bennet whispered it to me and she has not yet been to Meryton to tell anyone and of course Lady Lucas will be gone to Kent early in the morning tomorrow, so unless my sister drives to Lucas Lodge (which I do not believe she will, by the bye), no one will know of it but we two. Such a piece of news! Two pieces of news, in fact, and I have been wild to tell you.'

She took a breath and a mouthful of tea. Much-needed, I'll warrant. I am as fond of conversation as anybody, but never have I met two women who talk so incessantly as Mrs Philips and her sister. I eyed the rout cakes and decided against taking a third. By the time I finished my visit, went to the apothecary for some lavender water for my cook, Mrs Rumbold, and returned home, it would be time for luncheon and I did not wish to spoil my appetite. Mrs

Philips poured me a second cup of tea and sat forward, her hands clasped together and her face aglow with excitement.

'Jane is to have a child! And Lizzy too. Only to think, Mrs Long! Two grand-neices or nephews for me and two grandchildren for my sister and brother Bennet! They are expected around Christmas. Perhaps Lizzy will have a son who will inherit the great Pemberley estate! It does not matter quite so much if Jane should have a girl first, for Mr Bingley, as you know, only rents Netherfield Park and is yet to purchase his own estate. My sister tells me they are both in good health and there is no reason to be anxious about either of them. She visits the Bingleys at least three times a week and she will stay there when Jane expects her confinement and she and Mr Bennet and the girls are to spend a month complete in August in Derbyshire when the whole family party will be there. Mr Darcy's sister is still not engaged to a suitable gentleman, but she is yet full young and I am sure Lizzy will be glad enough of her company when the babe is born. Are not you diverted, my dear Mrs Long?'

I own that I was. I did not think that Mrs Bennet could long bear Lady Lucas' superiority in having a grandchild and now she expects two of her own. I finished my tea, bade my friend farewell and walked up the street, stopping to tell all my acquaintances the good news. Lady Lucas should have heard of it by nightfall, although of course Lizzy has probably written to Charlotte already.

A GREAT DEAL OF INGENUITY

†

The news that Mrs Bingley and Mrs Darcy were breeding encouraged me yet further to work on my own neices' marriage prospects. I found them sitting in the parlour engaged on their embroidery when I returned home. Dorothea is a very pretty girl, with regular features and naturally curling rich brown hair. Catherine is not a beauty, to be sure, but she has plenty of wit and vivacity and reads very widely. I will be excessively surprized if at least one of them is not married and settled by Christmas.

†

'I saw Mr Thomas Goulding this morning, aunt,' said Dorothea, as we ate our cold ham and pickles. 'He was riding along with his father and stopped to enquire after our health. They dine with us on Friday, do not they? I trust you will have three full courses?'

I assured her that I would. Mrs Rumbold has a light hand with pastry and is more than capable of providing a fine dinner, elegant enough even to please the Gouldings. Young Mr Goulding would be a fine match for my neice. I would be vastly happy to have her settled so close to me. Once the engagement has been announced, I can begin to search in earnest for a husband for Catherine.

I have taken care to invite the guests to my family dinner who will best advance Dorothea's interests. I am mindful that Mrs Bennet still has two daughters to dispose of in marriage and I would not be at all surprized if she had her eye on young Thomas Goulding.

The Bennets are not to be of the party. I noticed Mrs Bennet speaking to Lady Goulding at length over the supper table at the last assembly and having married three daughters in six months, she has finally got in the way of it. Dorothea is a hundred times prettier than Mary and Kitty Bennet and she will have six thousand pounds when she marries, a more alluring prospect to a young gentleman than one thousand pounds in the four per cents[63]. Still, I will be able to sleep comfortably in my bed once I can be sure that at least one of my neices has secured the hand of a respectable young man with a good fortune.

Mr and Mrs Morris will be of the party. They are most agreeable and while not particularly wealthy, extremely respectable. Their eldest son is Mr Philips' clerk. He might make a very suitable husband for Catherine if the oldest Lucas boy does not suit. I shall make sure that Catherine

---

[63] Mrs Long is being rather catty here. The Bennet girls will only have £1000 each in the four per cents whether they marry or not. The landed gentry of limited means, such as Mr Bennet, often invested their money in secure government bonds. There was little risk attached, but equally, little profit made. In spite of the elder girls' beauty, they had to marry wealthy men, as they will have only £40 per year and no home the second Mr Bennet's heart stops. In comparison, Mrs Long's nieces have larger dowries and their parents can expect their daughters to attract good matches as they can bring some wealth to the marriage. Additionally, there are only two of them so the money will go further. Mrs Bennet, the daughter of a country attorney, came to Longbourn House upon her marriage with only £4,000, not nearly enough to divide between five daughters and give them a decent settlement and certainly not enough to offset her new husband's alarming lack of cash. Mrs Bennet would know this, and perhaps it would go some way to explaining her apparent dislike of Mrs Long in the early part of the novel when excitement is at fever pitch with Mr Bingley's arrival at Netherfield Park.

takes particular care with her hair and dress on the night of my dinner.

†

Five and twenty years ago, when Miss Gardiner and Miss Maria Gardiner were still living at home with their mama and papa in the pretty house next to the parsonage, I was fortunate enough to catch the eye of Mr Charles Long, a most agreeable gentleman who had just come out of mourning for his wife. My sister had been married for two years and my mama was beginning to despair of ever finding me a husband when Mr Long moved into the neighbourhood. He had made a tolerable fortune in trade and having married a wealthy young lady from Essex had settled down with her to enjoy all the pleasures and benefits of matrimony. Her death, at the age of only one and twenty, while giving birth to her first child was a great grief to him, as can be imagined. Selling the small estate they had purchased upon their marriage and moving to Hertfordshire with his little daughter, he immediately became the cynosure[64] of all eyes. Young, handsome and wealthy, eager mamas were waiting only for him to put off his mourning clothes to begin introducing him to their marriageable daughters. It was fortunate for me that Mr Long had no interest in silly, giggling misses. We were introduced at the assemblies. He asked me to dance and

---

[64] A person who is the centre of attention for one reason or another (in this case because he is a wealthy widower).

during the set, we spoke of books, reading and the countryside. Three months later, we were married.

My husband was a rational and kindly gentleman. Our life together was unmarred by even a single cross word. His daughter I loved as my own and as the years went by and no children of our own came to bless us, never once did he reproach me as many other husbands would have done.

When Miss Henrietta Long was nineteen years old, I secured an excellent match for her. She is settled in Dorsetshire with a little boy of her own and another babe on the way. I travel down to see her as often as I can when I am not occupied with my neices and they are gone home. She is a most sweet and amiable young lady and her husband, a gentleman of wealth and property, doats upon her. If I do not secure a suitable match for Catherine this side of Christmas, I shall take her with me into Dorsetshire in the new year. Mrs Villiers (as she now is) dines with the entire county and her husband's wealth and consequence ensures that she moves in the very best social circles. If it were not such a long journey, I would take my neices there more often, but I own that I dread being so far from either of them. I miss my dear Henrietta more than I can say, but she is a most regular and faithful correspondent.

†

We spent a quiet evening at home, Dorothea playing and singing and Catherine reading and trimming a bonnet. I shall miss them both exceedingly when they are married or gone home to their mama.

A GREAT DEAL OF INGENUITY

Mrs Bennet, who was the liveliest and merriest of all of us in Meryton is now more ample in figure than she would wish to be. Five daughters in seven years was a sore trial to her, with no son to bring joy to his mother's heart and cut off the entail. It will be a strange day indeed when Mr Collins, his wife and children preside at Longbourn House. I would have wished to have my own babes, but my dear neices and Henrietta have brought me more happiness than most daughters do their mothers, I will warrant. And they have not destroyed my figure nor been responsible for the loss of my teeth. Poor Mrs Bennet in her flowing gowns and lace caps spends a deal of money on dress, but it is all for naught. The first bloom of youth has fled and will ne'er return. I, on the other hand, am strong and healthy, with all my own teeth, an excellent digestion and the strongest set of nerves in all of Hertfordshire. Which I shall require as I enter the lists for my neices in the marriage stakes.

Mrs Morris has only sons and is a very good sort of woman. Lady Goulding has five sons and five daughters and has married two of her girls out of the county. Lady Lucas has four daughters (one married, two out, one still in the school room) and Mrs Philips has no children. The Harrington girls are both of marriageable age and pretty enough, although nearly as silly as Miss Lydia used to be. I had wondered if there was an understanding between Harriet and one of the soldiers, but that has come to naught. What with Miss Kitty Bennet, who is tolerably handsome and Miss Mary who may yet blossom into good looks (although I doubt it, new gown or no new gown), there are nine young ladies in Meryton and Longbourn apart from my own neices who are searching for husbands.

A lesser woman would quail at the very thought, but never let it be said that Mary Ann Long is afraid of a challenge.

†

My dear husband married me for love. My four thousand pounds was certainly not his object as he had first married a wealthy woman and benefited from her fortune as well as his own. There were not many married couples in Meryton, I think, who were as well-matched and happy as we were. When he died of a fever five years ago, he left me a grief-stricken widow with a good house in an excellent position, a fine instrument in the parlour, a flock of poultry who lay all year round and a jointure[65] which allowed me to live well once I had left off mourning. I did not keep the chaise and pair in which I had dashed about in the first years of our marriage. I sold it for a good price and put the money prudently aside. Let Mrs Bennet sneer at the hack chaise which conveys me and the girls to dances. She has no security on which to depend as I do.

†

Friday evening came soon enough and I sent the girls up to dress two full hours before the guests were expected. My sister married a wealthy man and has provided me with more than enough money to ensure that her daughters are

---

[65] Monies and property settled upon a wife for use after her husband dies. Mrs Long brought a good dowry to her marriage and it is probably this which is giving her a comfortable and secure lifestyle.

exceedingly well-dressed as they hunt for husbands. Dorothea came downstairs in a white gown with Pomona Green[66] ornaments in the new, fashionable stile while her sister wore yellow, a colour which suits her complexion very well.

'If only your dear mama could see you! How proud she would be. I shall write to her directly to tell her of the latest news.'

My dear sister married well and moved to the county of Bedfordshire. She too was fortunate to find a husband who was kindly and well-bred, as well as tolerably wealthy and able to give her a comfortable home. All was well until her third confinement. She suffered from a childbed fever which settled in her lower limbs and rendered her lame and almost unable to walk. Her babe, a son, died two days after his birth and my afflicted sister was left a cripple, spending most of her day upon the sopha. Her husband employed an excessively well-bred and good natured governess for the girls who gave them a fine education but it was a great grief to their mother to be so incapacitated. In addition to her ills, their home is situated outside a very small village where they visit perhaps only eight families. When the girls came out, they met very few young gentlemen of marriageable age or suitable background and it was then that I offered my assistance.

My neices generally visit me in Meryton at least twice a year, staying for several months at a time. My sister and her husband travel to Bath and Cheltenham each year to take

---

[66] An extremely fashionable shade of green in Jane Austen's time. Yellow was also very popular.
Mrs Long's nieces are "on trend."

the waters and to seek a cure, so far, in vain. They are most generous with their wealth, giving me more than enough for the girls' board and pocket money. Even Mrs Bennet cannot say that her girls are better dressed than my neices, and *she* managed to catch men with five thousand and ten thousand pounds a year!

†

The candles lit and the dining parlour scented with posies of fresh flowers picked by the girls from the garden, I walked around the table one more time to ensure that all was in place. My cook is a treasure. She has been with me since the very first days of my marriage and is a most agreeable and hard-working woman. She never stands around gossiping in the street as so many of the other servants do. She too has a violent aversion to Mrs Nicholls, the cook at Netherfield House. I cannot speak ill of that woman's dishes, which are extremely good, but there is something about her manner which I find unpleasant. I would certainly not employ her in my own household whatever Lady Goulding has to say about her.

I sense that tonight may be the night that young Mr Goulding's affection tips over into a formal application for Dorothea's hand. With that in mind, I have seated her next to him and laid in a stock of particularly good claret and port. Young Mr Goulding's father is fond of the good things of the table and rapidly becomes affable and garrulous under the influence of strong drink.

I heard the sound of the Gouldings' four well-matched horses' hooves clip-clopping to a stop outside my front door. A moment or two later, the bell rang. In they all came, Mr William Goulding in his best suit of clothes, boots polished and gold buttons gleaming (although straining somewhat over his well-fed stomach, I could not but help notice), Lady Goulding with her fine clothes and lined face, young Mr Thomas Goulding with a high colour and eager eyes seeking out my neice, and the two oldest Goulding daughters. My little maid Polly (such a good and cheerful girl!) brought them into the drawing room where a tray of glasses and a decanter of good claret was waiting. I was cheered to notice that young Mr Goulding immediately engaged Dorothea in conversation and the two of them walked over to the window and spoke in low voices. The bell rang again, and again, and soon our party was assembled.

My elegant family dinner was a triumph! Mrs Rumbold excelled herself. The dish of dressed cucumbers, lettuce and tomatoes (from our own kitchen garden) pleased even Mr Goulding and the roasted pigeons were done to a turn. We enjoyed veal cutlets with a caper sauce, new potatoes, poached salmon, asparagus and radishes, and Mrs Rumbold's apple tart with thick cream was universally praised. What a mollifying effect good food can have on even the most nervous of persons. Lady Goulding's face relaxed as the meal went on, and by the time she was enjoying her second dish of apple tart, she was positively radiant. I too was encouraged to hope that her son would soon be paying me a morning visit to ask for my neice's hand. He spoke to no one else during dinner and afterwards, when the girls were pouring out coffee in the parlour, hovered about Dorothea as though anxious to protect her from the evil designs of other young gentlemen.

Never let it be said that Mary Ann Long is able only to do one thing at a time. Assured of Mr Goulding's preference for Dorothea, I kept a sharp eye on young Mr Morris, Mr Philips' clerk. He is a tall young man of about four and twenty with a ready wit. I made sure to overhear his conversation with Catherine at dinner over the veal cutlets and was delighted to realise that they were talking of books. My dear neice is even better-read than Miss Mary Bennet and far better looking. Even if Mrs Bennet had her eye on Mr Morris for one of her daughters (and I am sure she does), my dinner has sparked a most promising affection in him for young Catherine. After dinner, over coffee, they were as deep in conversation as Dorothea and Mr Thomas Goulding. Watching the candlelight reflect off the best glassware and strike deep notes of auburn and chestnut from Dorothea's hair, I reflected with pleasure how much joy it would give me to greet Lady Lucas upon her return with the news that I had not one, but two neices engaged to be married.

†

The next morning dawned fine and just after we had breakfasted, the front door bell rang. I had taken care to advise Dorothea to dress in her most becoming gown and got her up half an hour early to have her hair done in the new stile. Polly is become a good little lady's maid. I may have to reconcile myself to her departure when Dorothea is married as she is sure to want to take her with her to Haye-

Park. Sure enough, there was a knock on the morning room door and Polly announced Mr Thomas Goulding, still ruddy-cheeked from his precipitate dash on horseback from his ancestral home. The girls were upstairs, leaving me to manage the business which would have been my husband's responsibility had a merciful God decided to spare him.

Within five minutes, all was settled. Mr Goulding told me of his violent affection for Dorothea and his desire to make her his wife before the year was out. Having already secured my brother and sister's consent, all that was left to me was to call Miss Dorothea down and leave them alone together in the morning room while I spoke to Mrs Rumbold in the kitchen about the rhubarb tarts for next week's supper party.

†

Our home is a whirl of excitement! My dear Dorothea is glowing with happiness and sat down at once to write to her dear papa and mama. I too wrote to them to express my joy at the forthcoming nuptials and to engage them for a full description of the settlement they would make upon my neice. Once the business was concluded, I put on my light pelisse and second-best bonnet and hurried out to walk to Longbourn House and tell Mrs Bennet the good news. It would not do to allow her to hear it from another. On my way, should I meet any of my other friends, I will of course vouchsafe the glad tidings. Before dinner, I will write to Lady Lucas in Kent so that she does not feel that she has missed an announcement of such importance.

I wonder how Charlotte goes on. I shall walk to Lucas Lodge tomorrow morning after breakfast to see if there is any news.

✝

My brother has written with details of what he will give Dorothea and what she may spend on her clothes. He is the most generous of men. Mr Thomas Goulding dines with us every night. He cannot bear to be separated from his fiancée which is just as I would wish. They go on very well together. We are invited to the Philips for supper next week. The Bennets will be there of course, all the Gouldings, the Morrises, the Harringtons and Sir William Lucas with Miss Louisa. We will meet again at the Netherfield ball in July. Mr Bingley is most generous with his hospitality and Mr Morris is sure to ask Catherine for at least two dances. Who can resist falling in love in a ballroom, especially one as grand and splendid as the one at Netherfield Park, lit with thousands of wax candles. The musicians will be brought direct from London, I will wager, and the supper table will be groaning with elegant viands[67].

I will make sure that Catherine and Mr Morris have ample opportunity to talk at the Philips'. Mrs Bennet may be able to produce a daughter who reads as much as my neice, but not one with nearly so much wit and flow to her conversation. Catherine is not a great card player, unlike Mrs Bennet and Kitty. While they win and lose fish in their interminable games of lottery tickets, I shall be advancing

---

[67] An archaic word for food.

the future of my girl. With no children of their own, I wonder if Mr Philips intends to bequeath his business to his clerk. I shall introduce the subject with his wife over coffee next time I call upon her.

†

News from Kent! Charlotte has had a fine, large boy, who made his appearance at supper time on the very day that Lady Lucas and Maria arrived at the parsonage! He is thriving and she is doing well, although Lady Lucas writes that at one point, she was despaired of. She is weak and tired, but recovering apace. Mr Collins is delighted with his son and Lady Catherine de Bourgh herself has paid a visit to the parsonage to view him and look over the arrangements for the guests from Hertfordshire. Lady Lucas will stay two more weeks before travelling home. Maria will stay on in Hunsford to help her sister for another month complete.

In her last letter to me, Lady Lucas mentioned a young gentleman who has visited the parsonage. Unmarried young ladies of good family are thin on the ground in Hunsford, it seems. I am perfectly well aware that this young man, whoever he might be, does not have the remotest interest in Charlotte or her baby.

I hope that Lady Lucas has taken my advice to dress Maria in stronger colours and to avoid green at all costs. No gentleman wishes to speak to a young lady who looks as though she is in the final stages of consumption!

†

Lady Goulding has paid me two morning visits to talk about wedding clothes and carriages and pin money and other delightful subjects. She is vastly pleased with her son's match and Dorothea has never been in better looks. At dinner with the Bennets at Longbourn on Tuesday evening, young Mr Goulding made no attempt at conversation with any body around the supper table. He only has eyes for his beloved.

Mrs Bennet was shooting sour looks at Catherine and Mr Morris. It may have been the effects of the gooseberry fool (just a touch too tart in my opinion – more sugar was wanted), but I do believe that she was thinking of him for one of her own daughters. I do not feel any sympathy for her. After all, I did not grudge Jane her splendid match with Mr Bingley even though I had hoped to attach his attentions to one of my neices. Mrs Bennet has only two daughters out of five left to dispose of in marriage and she can visit Pemberley any time she wishes where the Darcys move in the most exalted circles. If I were her, I would leave Mary and Kitty there for a month or two, chaperoned by Lizzy, and available for any young gentleman of fortune and good family to look over. Pickings in Meryton are slim now that Dorothea has captured Mr Thomas Goulding and the regiment are gone to Brighton.

A GREAT DEAL OF INGENUITY

†

We are engaged to dine with Mr and Mrs Morris next Monday, and we are bidden to Haye-Park for an intimate family dinner with the Gouldings this Friday. I own that I very much enjoy the hurly burly of socialising, drinking tea, playing cards and listening to music in the neighbourhood. How fortunate I am to live in such a thriving town as Meryton.

What I shall do when I have the girls safely married I do not know.

After breakfast, I set out to walk to Lucas Lodge to see how Sir William and Louisa go on. Little Betsey is still in the school room (and at ten years old shewing more promise of beauty than any of her sisters) and the boys away at school. Sir William is driving to Hunsford to collect Lady Lucas and see his grandson next week. The governess will chaperone Miss Louisa and Betsey in his absence.

I walked up the drive of Lucas Lodge noticing as I did so that there are the beginnings of weeds encroaching on the flower beds and that the gravel has not been raked for several days. The gardener is a lazy fellow and without Lady Lucas at home to observe what goes on, he is taking a holiday.

Sir William has a numerous family for whom to provide and he quit his business too early in life in my opinion. His knighthood and the self-importance it gave him led him to behave rashly. He is fortunate to have married his eldest daughter so well and I hope for his sake that Lady Lucas and Charlotte between them can manage to secure a match for Maria in Kent. If I did not have the girls to attend to, I would offer to visit Hunsford myself as I flatter myself that I can fan the spark of a slight preference into the raging flames of love with no difficulty at all. Charlotte had to do all the work to secure Mr Collins. Her mother had nothing to do with it at all, so Mrs Philips tells me.

I found Miss Louisa in the breakfast room finishing her cup of chocolate and buttering a roll lavishly. With her mother from home, late hours are being kept at Lucas Lodge. She has known me all her life and did not seem alarmed or surprized at such an early call. Lady Lucas would never have shewn me any of her correspondence had she been at home, but I had spied a letter lying on the table and I had every intention of reading it for myself before Mrs Philips and Mrs Bennet had heard all about the news contained within it.

'Have you heard from your mama lately, my dear?' I enquired, taking off my bonnet and complimenting her on her new gown (a most frightful colour! Young ladies of Miss Louisa's complexion should never wear light blue. But we must always observe good manners in such a small and enclosed society).

'Why yes, Mrs Long. Papa received a long letter from Mama this morning. I have just finished reading it.'

A young girl of sixteen years is no match for Mary Ann Long. I smiled encouragingly at her and she duly passed the letter to me. I devoured the thrilling contents greedily. Charlotte goes on well, the babe is hearty and thriving, Lady Catherine de Bourgh, Miss Anne de Bourgh and Mrs Jenkinson have visited the parsonage three times, the fox got into the poultry houses and ate up five of the pullets, a Mr Simpson called and drank tea with the family party at the parsonage, Mr Potts the apothecary has visited Rosings Park twice with draughts for Lady Catherine who is suffering with pains in her chest, the monthly nurse[68] is insolent and impertinent in Lady Lucas' opinion, Mr Simpson is coming for dinner on Thursday and Lady Lucas asks that some more of Maria's gowns and hair ornaments be packed up and sent to Hunsford.

As I suspected, matters are moving on apace in Kent. I shall question Lady Lucas when she returns and find out more of Mr Simpson, his family background, his situation and the degree of his prosperity. In Meryton, Miss Lucas has the pretty faces of the Harrington girls, Miss Kitty Bennet and my own dear Catherine with which to compete. In Hunsford, with only poor Charlotte recently risen from the toils of childbed and Lady Lucas who, even in her first bloom, could only ever be described as a "fine girl," the little beauty she does have will be in evidence. It is remarkable what the right gown and ornaments and candlelight can do for a young girl. What a pity it is that there is unlikely to be any dancing at Hunsford! I am quite sure that young Mr Morris will ask my Catherine for at least two dances at the Netherfield ball and as every eager mama (and aunt) knows, love often blossoms in a ballroom.

---

[68] This was a nurse who looked after a new mother and her baby for around four weeks following birth. Women of Charlotte Collins' class would rest in bed and stay at home for a prolonged period after childbirth with their mother or mother-in-law in attendance if possible. Once this time was over, the woman would be reintroduced into society with a ceremony called the churching of women at her local church (in this case it would be conducted by Mr Collins). It may well be that wealthy Lady Catherine has paid for the monthly nurse who is reporting back to her on how things are going at the parsonage.

†

Dinner at the Morrises was delightful. They keep a very good cook and served two full courses. The partridges were done to a turn and I very much enjoyed the cherry tart with cream. More pleasing even than the anchovy sauce with the roast lamb was the way in which young Mr Morris engaged Catherine in conversation during dinner and over coffee. He produced three of his own books and pressed her to take them home, saying that he was sure they would be to her taste. Dorothea sang and played and Miss Mary Bennet insisted on playing several sonatas very ill immediately afterwards. Miss Kitty giggled and simpered in the corner and stared at young Mr Henry Morris. He will not suit. She is far too silly and frivolous for him and Mrs Morris would never countenance such a match.

I took the opportunity of telling Mrs Bennet the news from Hunsford. She was most relieved to hear that Miss Maria Lucas seems to have attracted the attentions of a young man. We have known each other for so many years that I could see her counting off the remaining fair rivals to her own daughters in Meryton in her head. If all goes to plan in Kent, I calculate that there will be only seven unmarried young ladies left in our neighbourhood. Six, if Mr Morris proposes to Catherine before she returns home. If it should come to naught, I shall suggest that I take her to Dorsetshire in the new year where she is sure to meet a suitable young man.

'And of course, my dear, if Maria Lucas *does* make a match with this Mr Simpson, that will be two of the girls married and settled in Kent. Lady Lucas is sure to pay more visits with Louisa who is full young to be thinking of marriage yet to be sure, but her sisters can chaperone her and it may very well be that *she* will find a suitable husband in Kent too. Do you know if Pen Harrington's cough is any better? She looked very pale at my sister Philips'. And those turkey-red ribbons do not suit her at all. I wonder if Lady Lucas is dressing Maria any better. As I always say to my sister Gardiner, it is vastly important to dress a young lady in the new stile when there are gentlemen to be met. And are you pleased with Dorothea's match, my dear? To be sure, Haye-Park is not as modern or spacious as Netherfield, but it has a pleasant prospect and the Gouldings are very good sorts of people and vastly respectable.'

She broke off to reach for a liberally buttered rout cake and glanced over at Mary, who was playing a concerto in spite of the chatter rising all around her.

'That colour suits Mary very well,' I observed with some magnanimity. With one neice engaged and another much admired by a suitable young man, I was in no humour to gloat and could afford to be generous with my compliments.

'Now that Jane, Lizzy and Lydia are married and settled, your maid must have more time to dress the girls' hair. That stile is most becoming to Mary's face. And of course, Kitty is very pretty indeed.'

Mrs Bennet's face was wreathed in smiles as she wiped melted butter from her chin.

'Thank you, my dear Mrs Long. And your neices are very pretty-behaved girls. Most amiable and unpretending. I was saying to my sister Philips the other day, Miss

Dorothea will do very well with young Mr Goulding. Very well indeed.'

I seized the opportunity to enquire after Mrs Wickham, living a rackety life in Newcastle by all accounts.

'My dear, dear Lydia! She is prodigiously happy; indeed she is! Such a charming husband. He has the most delightful manners and *so* handsome! But you will understand, Mrs Long. We were both very fond of a red coat when we were young, were not we?'

She giggled and for a moment I could almost fancy that I saw pretty, carefree Miss Gardiner in front of me again.

Mary finished her concerto and there were cries for Dorothea to return to the instrument and to play some lively airs. With all the news shared, I had little left to do except to bask in the happy glow of complaisance at having made an excellent match for one neice and perhaps begun the work of a second one. Mr Morris and Catherine were sitting quietly together on a sopha, a little apart from the others and were engaged in conversation. To my surprize, I felt my eyes moisten as I remembered sitting on a sopha at the Gardiners' five and twenty years before, listening to Mr Long speak of books and feeling myself falling in love.

If I could be sure that my girls will be half as happy as I was in marriage, I will die a happy woman.

Not that I intend to die for quite some time yet! I am as sure as I can be that Mrs Wickham is not half so happy as her mother believes her to be and I need to remain hale and hearty so that I may hear and disseminate all the news and gossip in Meryton.

Will Miss Maria Lucas secure a match with the mysterious Mr Simpson? Will Lady Lucas dispose of three out of four of her daughters in Kent? Who will marry the Harrington sisters? Will Mrs Bennet descend to the level of a Lucas sprig in order to marry off her remaining daughters? How many more children will that oily Mr Collins get on his poor wife? What is the nature of the chest pains from which Lady Catherine de Bourgh is suffering? What stile of bonnet and veil will best become Dorothea on her wedding day? Can I acquire the receipt[69] for rout cakes from Mrs Philips' cook before the year is out?

Watching my girls in the soft candlelight, my heart swelled with pride. Although I have never been blessed with my own children, I love my neices as though they were my own.

Tomorrow, I shall walk to Lucas Lodge after breakfast to call on Sir William and Louisa and see if another letter is come from Kent. It is devoutly to be hoped that Mr Simpson is an impetuous and warm-hearted young man and that Maria Lucas' pallid charms have won his heart. This being the case, I will be the first to know of it and to take the opportunity of telling everyone in Meryton the good news.

I wonder what Mrs Bennet will have to say.

---

[69] Recipe

A Fine Trousseau

Mrs Bennet is one of the best-known characters in literature with her nerves, her violent fidgets, her five unmarried daughters and her passion for visiting and news. However, she is also one of the three children of the deceased Mr and Mrs Gardiner and as well as an older brother (uncle to the Bennet girls, married to the amiable and well-bred Mrs Gardiner), she has a sister Philips, married to an attorney and living in Meryton. This book started with the elder Miss Gardiner and it seemed only right to complete it with the younger, "Miss Maria" from the first story. We are told that Miss Maria married her father's clerk and there is no mention of any children. It may well be that she is living in her childhood home and she has certainly not strayed very far from her roots. She too is fond of visiting and news, often hosting her sister's family at her house and walking to Longbourn. She is first mentioned in Chapter 7 when Austen sketches out the Bennet girls' family background. Meryton and Longbourn are only one mile apart, a convenient walk for regular visits. Mr Philips visits all the officers so her house is a convenient and welcoming hub for the girls with its instrument, generous hospitality and enough room for *impromptu dancing. Mrs Hurst and Miss Bingley have some cutting remarks to make about Mr Philips' relatively humble profession while Jane is ill at Netherfield and Mrs Philips is not the most discreet of women as we learn in Chapter 55. No sooner have Jane and Bingley got engaged than Mrs Bennet has told her sister. 'Mrs Bennet was privileged to whisper it to Mrs Philips, and <u>she</u> ventured, without any permission, to do the same by all her neighbours in Meryton.' She is a sociable woman, throwing her house open to the officers, her neighbours and families and having the pleasure of having her drawing room compared to a small summer breakfast parlour at Rosings by Mr Collins. The apple doesn't fall far from the tree and in Chapter 60, we learn that Mr Darcy is exposed to Mrs Philips' "vulgarity" during his engagement to Elizabeth. Miss Gardiner, the pretty, merry, marriageable girl started this book off, and her less conventionally attractive and more outspoken sister is going to bring it to a close.*

BLESS ME, what a great deal has happened in a short space of time. As I was saying to my sister Bennet just the other day when calling upon her at Longbourn, who would have believed that she would have got rid of three of the girls in less than a twelvemonth? Jane married and settled at Netherfield Park, Lizzy up in Derbyshire and the grandest of them all and my little Lydia living in Newcastle and the pet of all the officers, if her letters are to be believed.

My parlour looks directly out on to the street and many are the times I have thrown up the window and called out to my neices as they walked past with the Lucases and the Harrington girls. I am a respectable woman of rapidly advancing years but my heart still beat a little faster as I watched Colonel Forster and his men march up the street in their regimentals in the spring. My sister was always very fond of a red coat when we were girls and it is such an outfit matched with a handsome face and charming manners that has whisked my youngest neice, Lydia, off to Newcastle to live the life of a soldier's wife. I still remember Colonel Miller dining with us when Mama and Papa were yet spared to us and my sister Bennet flirting tenderly with him over the cold ham and boiled potatoes.

My dear neices have been more like daughters to me. When I was a girl in Meryton, I would make clothes for my dolls from scraps of cloth and dream of becoming a mother myself. My brother Gardiner and his wife have given me two neices and two nephews and my sister Bennet five more, but it has not pleased God to send Mr Philips and me children of our own. As winter comes upon us and the fire in the parlour is heaped up, I find myself often sitting in my chair with my work forgotten in my lap dreaming of what might have been.

†

As the youngest of three living children, I should have been the pet, as Miss Lydia is to my sister Bennet. From my earliest recollections, however, it was my sister who was the favourite in our house, preferred by Papa and spoiled by

A GREAT DEAL OF INGENUITY

Mama. My brother Gardiner was a boy of ten when I was born, too old to be a true companion to me, and my sister is but two years older than myself. Our other brothers and sisters had not staid long upon this earth, to Mama's great grief.

Papa was the attorney in Meryton, a respectable profession, and we lived in a comfortable house next to the parsonage. One of my earliest memories is Mama sitting in the parlour looking out upon her neighbours and calling out to them through the window. We dined with quite eight and twenty families and Mama was a most hospitable woman who kept a very good table. My sister, with her rich brown curls, bright blue eyes and fine complexion was a favourite with all who knew her. Pert and noisy, she would dance and sing for all who came to the house, while I, the quieter, plainer sister was kept back, in spite of my superior accomplishments. As I grew older, my glass told me that I had no beauty to speak of. I saw Mama's disappointment in my thin figure and plain face every day and my sister, while never unkind, did not become the intimate companion for whom I longed.

†

As we grew older, our lives changed. My sister had come out and I was forced to stay at home with the servant and watch as she capered around the parlour in her new dress, dancing shoes and hair ornaments, ready to attend the dance at the assemblies.

'I am wild to dance, Maria!' cried she, sinking down upon the sopha and clapping her gloved hand to her heart.

'I long to hear the musicians and make new acquaintances. Mama says that a girl's first dance will often fix the affection of several young men. And once I am engaged, you know, you can come out and we may attend balls together. To be sure, the company is pretty thin, but perhaps there will be a rich gentleman there, with four or five thousand pounds a year and a fine estate who may wish to be introduced to me. And if not, Colonel Miller and his men in their fine red coats will make delightful dancing partners, will they not?'

I said nothing. I have found it best to ignore my sister's effusions. What rich young man would be tempted to pay court to a girl who would have only four thousand pounds and who was the daughter of a country attorney? I had seen the elegant carriages of the gentry parade down the street in Meryton often enough, with their liveried footmen and their perfectly matched horses and I could only dream of the grandeur and splendour of their houses.

I was glad enough when the hack chaise came to take Mama, Papa and my sister to the assemblies and I was left to my own company. I ran into the kitchen and begged a handful of barley sugar from the cook, then threw myself on the sopha and read my book. I much preferred more solitary pursuits to the noisy transports of my sister, plunged for the first time into polite society.

†

The year wore on and by Christmas, it was plain that while my sister danced every dance and was much admired at the balls and assemblies she attended, none of her dancing partners shewed a promising affection for her nor were rich enough to tempt her into matrimony. One morning, we were sitting in the parlour while Mama enumerated the virtues of the single gentlemen in the neighbourhood.

'What a pity, my dear, that Mr William Lucas is married already. He is in a fair way to become very rich from his business and he has a fine house.'

My sister pouted.

'He has that tribe of children already – and they are so plain! I hope you noticed them in church on Sunday, Maria. The eldest girl pale and thin just like her mother and those two boys so coarse and clumsy. I would not have married him even had he been single.'

'Mr Jones the apothecary danced two dances with you at the assemblies, my dear. He is not the most handsome gentleman, but he is respectable and he could offer you a comfortable home. Or Mr Henry Clarke. When his father dies, he will inherit the library and they have a good income. His mother drives about in a very smart carriage and they are very agreeable, well-bred people.'

A loud sigh indicated what Miss Gardiner thought of her suitors.

'But they are all so dull, Mama! I have known them for an age. I do not want to become like Mrs Lucas, having a child every year and sitting out reels and quadrilles to gossip at the supper table with all the other matrons. I long to marry a man in regimentals. Colonel Miller is a single man and he must have three or four thousand pounds a year, as well as being wildly handsome and fond of dancing.'

Mama pursed her lips.

'No daughter of mine will marry a soldier. It is no life for a respectable young lady, moving around the country and putting up in cramped lodgings. Colonel Miller may continue to dine with us but you are to put all thoughts of marriage to him, or any young man in uniform, out of your head!'

My sister pouted again, sulked, and threw a half-trimmed bonnet to the floor. She was not accustomed to being thwarted.

Mama stood up and adjusted her cap.

'Well, well, my dear, you are very young and there is yet time. Perhaps we should pay a visit to Edward up in town. You may catch the eye of a wealthy gentleman in trade. If a respectable merchant with four or five thousand pounds a year should want you, I should not say nay and neither would your papa.'

I stretched and gave a violent yawn. I was tired of the constant chatter about young gentlemen, carriages and finery.

'Shall not we go out to take a turn through Meryton, sister?" I asked. "At breakfast, Papa said he had business to conclude. Might not he be persuaded to take us with him?'

Mama had no objection and, pausing only to fuss over my sister's gown and to ensure her curls peeked prettily from under her new bonnet, she waved us off as we walked down the street. Although it was January, the weather was fine, with a gentle breeze and watery winter sunshine struggling through the clouds. My sister, I own, was looking at her very best, bewitchingly pretty with her sparkling eyes and merry face. Papa was to leave us at the haberdashers where we wished to look over some lace which had lately come in.

As we approached the shop, I heard my sister whispering to our father.

'Papa, who is that gentleman approaching us? Are you acquainted with him?'

Looking up, I saw a tolerably handsome gentleman with dark hair and a serious face walking towards us. He was smartly dressed and quite unknown to me. Upon seeing us, he smiled and bowed. Papa introduced us both and I watched as my sister fixed her eyes on our new acquaintance's face then dropped her eyelashes and blushed.

I wondered how much he had a year.

†

Mr Bennet (for such was the gentleman's name), was a most respectable gentleman with a tolerable fortune and a small estate not a mile from Meryton. He dined with us three times and looked to be falling very much in love with my sister. I did not think they will suit. He was of a serious disposition and I noticed him frown more than once when he thought I was not looking. However, Mama thought that it would be a match, her elder daughter married at seventeen and the mistress of Longbourn House. I wished them both joy. What else could I do? No one was interested in *my* opinion.

†

The fire wants poking and my cap has slipped to one side. I must have dozed off. I was dreaming I held a babe in my arms, its little head resting in the crook of my arm and its gentle breathing lifting its tiny chest up and down beneath its gown. Even now, many years after I knew that I would never be a mother, the dreams yet come.

It was three and twenty years ago I stood behind my sister and Mr Bennet as they made their vows in Meryton church. Our house was quieter once only Mama, Papa and me were left in it and Mama began to turn her attention to my future happiness and establishment.

'With a curl in your hair and some pretty new gowns, you will do very well, my dear. Edward is visiting us soon from London and I have written to him to beg him to bring the latest silks, muslins and patterns from his warehouses. You will be the most fashionably dressed young lady in Meryton!'

She stood behind me and touched my arm with her fingertips as the maid tortured my dead straight locks with the curling irons and the smell of scorched hair filled the room. I had just come out and was to attend the assemblies with Mama to see if I could catch the eye of a respectable young gentleman. It seemed unlikely. While my figure was formed and my features regular, I had none of the beauty or vivacity exhibited by my sister.

†

A twelvemonth went by. My sister Bennet presented her husband with a daughter, Jane. Mrs Lucas gave birth to her fourth child and third son. Mr Jones the apothecary wed a Miss Hammond of St Albans, a silly, empty-headed woman with a good fortune. Mary Ann Russell, who was no prettier than I, captivated a rich widower with a little daughter. I sat out more dances at the assemblies than I had partners and I longed to escape from the stifling society of Meryton. Even a visit to my brother Gardiner's house in town brought me no joy in the search for a suitable husband. Mama took to loudly sighing each time we climbed into the carriage to drive to a dance or ball. I pretended not to notice.

†

Five years after my sister's wedding to Mr Bennet, we were drinking tea at Longbourn and admiring my neices Jane, Elizabeth and Mary (named for me). My brother Bennet is become more silent and less amiable and the frown which I noticed in his courting days is a feature of his countenance more often than not. My sister expects a fourth babe; this one, she is sure, a boy to cut off the entail and secure the family's future. Jane is a delightfully pretty child, quiet and sweet with biddable manners. Elizabeth is livelier and chatters excitedly whenever company is come. Mary favours me in looks, as her mother sourly remarks, but it is of no import as her older sisters will surely marry well with their looks and charm.

My sister Bennet's eyes no longer sparkle as they once did (except when she has gone into Meryton and bought yet another length of material for a new gown) and her once glossy curls are dull now, confined within the lace cap of a married woman. Still, she has formed a friendship with Mrs Lucas whose growing brood often come to visit at Longbourn and play with her girls. She is wild for visiting and news and I have noticed a peevish tone creeping into her merry voice.

I sat on the sopha and held little Mary in my arms. She gazed earnestly into my face and played with my locket. Her eyes are wide-set and brown like my own. What kind of woman will she become; I wonder?

†

Time wore on. My sister Bennet had a fourth daughter, Kitty and then a fifth, Lydia. No son has come to bless Longbourn and to cut off the entail. My brother Gardiner is married to an elegant woman six years his junior from the county of Derbyshire. She is to have her first babe in the summer. I am become a plain old maid, good only for holding Mama's silk skeins as she embroiders yet more caps and gowns for her granddaughters and for giving my sister Bennet the company for which she longs.

Papa has a new clerk, a Mr Philips. He is all of eight and twenty, not at all handsome, with a broad face and a great fondness for good port wine. He dines with us at least once a week. He is at least respectable and tolerably agreeable. I can see Mama calculating how much we would require to set up housekeeping as she passes the potatoes to him. Toying with my syllabub, I allow my mind to wander. To be sure, I am not in the least in love with Mr Philips, but no better prospect offers and I cannot bear the thought of being Miss Gardiner for the rest of my life.

†

One morning, Mama invited me to join her in the parlour after breakfast.

'Now, my dear, Mr Philips has spoken to your father. He is in love with you and wishes to make you an offer of marriage. He is a very respectable young man from a good family and he could offer you a comfortable home. Church Cottage is empty, I know, and it has two good rooms downstairs and a large back kitchen. To be sure, it is rather cramped, but as he progresses in his work and as children come, you can move to a larger house. What say you, my dear? Could you love him? Could you see yourself becoming his wife?'

I gazed out of the window where the morning parade of Meryton matrons and their children had already begun. Mrs Lucas walked slowly past, her gown swelling at the front with yet another child and a brood of pale-faced little children running along behind her skirts. Mrs Long swept past in her carriage in her fine new silks and bonnet en route to the haberdasher's. Mrs Hayes waved from her chaise and pair, her hands full of parcels.

Certainly, I could see myself becoming Mr Philips' wife. I could see the cramped cottage, the low ceilings and the small garden, but I could also hear the greetings of my fellow matrons and see the envy in my sister's eyes as she looked through my fine trousseau. With a brother in trade in London and his warehouses full of bolts of silk, muslin, and lace, I should be as well dressed as my sister.

And after all, happiness in marriage is entirely a matter of chance. My sister Bennet captivated her husband with her youth and beauty and now he laughs at her and makes sport of her nerves in front of her children. Mama and Papa are grown old and lined with the work of bringing up three children and maintaining respectability in the town. My sister Gardiner, as yet merry and light of foot, will likely be a sour-faced matron before ten years have passed. What better chance will there be for Miss Maria Gardiner of Meryton?

Mama was looking anxious. She leaned forward and pressed my hand.

'Well, my dear? Do you? Do you think you could love Mr Philips and accept his offer of marriage?'

I thought of how my sister Bennet would look when she learned that her younger sister was finally to be married, with a house in Meryton and all the importance and consequence of a respectable matron, and made my decision.

'I do.'

Bibliography

Austen, Jane. *Pride and Prejudice*. Penguin Classics, 1996.

Baker, Jo. *Longbourn*. Transworld Publishers, 2013.

Byrne, Paula. *The Real Jane Austen: A Life in Small Things*. William Collins, 2013.

Coolidge, Susan. *What Katy Did Next*. Puffin Classics, 1994. Originally published 1886.

Greeley, Molly. *The Clergyman's Wife*. William Morrow, 2019.

Hadlow, Janice. *The Other Bennet Sister*. Mantle, 2020.

Kelly, Helena. *Jane Austen The Secret Radical*. Icon Books Ltd, 2016.

Mullan, John. *What Matters In Jane Austen?* Bloomsbury, 2012

Porter, Joanna. *A Governess in the Age of Jane Austen: The Journals and Letters of Agnes Porter* (edited by Joanna Martin). The Hambledon Press, 1998.

Servitova, Rose. *The Longbourn Letters*. Wooster Publishing, 2017.

Sutherland, John. *Who Betrays Elizabeth Bennet?* Oxford World's Classics, 1999.

Tomalin, Claire. *Jane Austen: A Life.* Penguin Books Ltd, 1997.

Holy Bible: King James (Authorised) Version. Collins, UK.

I'm indebted to Laurel Ann Nattress at Austenprose, Austenopedia and The Republic of Pemberley Pride and Prejudice E-Text.

Also By This Author

The Diary of Isabella M Smugge (Instant Apostle) – available at www.ruthleighwrites.co.uk and all good online bookstores

The Trials of Isabella M Smugge (Instant Apostle) – available at www.ruthleighwrites.co.uk and all good online bookstores

The Continued Times of Isabella M Smugge (Instant Apostle) – available at www.ruthleighwrites.co.uk and all good online bookstores

Printed in Great Britain
by Amazon